THE MANLY ART

I grinned at him. "Good evening."

"I seen you watching me. Didn't recognize you at first," he said.

"At least we aren't going to have to pretend we never met before," I told him.

Blair laughed. "I know you well enough, man. Well enough to whip your ass a second time."

"Are you getting paid for this one too?"

"It's going to be my pleasure, man. My pleasure."

I wasn't going to turn my back on the bastard a second time.

Wasn't going to trust him to play by the Marquess of Queensbury rules, either.

Blair reached a patch of deep shadow, planted his foot in the middle of seemingly normal stride, and spun around with a real haymaker that was armed and dangerous.

If I hadn't been expecting something of the sort it would have plucked my head clean off my shoulders. Which was exactly what old Henry was wanting.

I bobbed to the left to let the punch pull him off balance, stepped inside it, and popped him a quick combination over the kidney.

It felt like hitting one of those slabs of hanging beef in *Rocky*. I wasn't sure that I hadn't hurt myself more than I did him. Mr. Blair was in excellent condition indeed.

He cussed me enough to start a whole new fight and began bobbing and weaving the way a talented amateur boxer will.

"Had yourself some lessons in the manly art, Henry? Let me give you another."

Other Carl Heller novels by Frank Roderus
Ask your bookseller for the books you have missed

THE OIL RIG
THE RAIN RUSTLERS

A HELLER NOVEL

THE VIDEO VANDAL
Frank Roderus

BANTAM BOOKS
TORONTO • NEW YORK • LONDON • SYDNEY • AUCKLAND

THE VIDEO VANDAL

A Bantam Book / November 1984

ISBN 0-553-24499-X

Published simultaneously in the United States and Canada

Bantam Books are published by Bantam Books, Inc. Its trademark,
consisting of the words "Bantam Books" and the portrayal of a
rooster, is Registered in U.S. Patent and Trademark Office and in
other countries. Marca Registrada. Bantam Books, Inc., 666 Fifth
Avenue, New York, New York 10103.

PRINTED IN THE UNITED STATES OF AMERICA

H   0 9 8 7 6 5 4 3 2 1

For Jim Menick

1

I went to sleep with it every night and woke up with it every morning. Fell asleep to the sound of popping soft-wood embers and the soughing of wind in the trees and the horses cropping grass. And to the memory of a woman I would never see again. Woke up to the chill of the early morning and a hollow place in my belly that yearned for coffee and to the impatient stamping of the horses on their picket ropes. And to the knowledge that I didn't even know where her body was buried.

The weeks of solitude in the high country, far from human contact or social convention, had done nothing to dispel my moods, and I began to wonder if I should instead have gone on a long and busy drunk. I doubted that, though. I'd make a lousy drunk.

But then, it seemed I was a flop as a solitary mountain man too. Those old-timers had been hearty and self-sufficient, at peace with the land around them if not always with its inhabitants. Me, I was just a wanderer with a load of self-pity on his shoulders so heavy that I was no longer seeing the country I rode through.

I had entered the public land at my ranch north of Lake George and hadn't seen a fence or another human—not close enough to talk to anyhow—since then. I'd ridden across the minor peaks and around the major ones until I could see the lights of Denver far below and far away and then turned back into the mountains, not wanting anyone's laughter or happiness to intrude on my self-condemnation.

Oh, I was in a fine, black mood, and I was milking it for all it was worth and then some. Poor, poor pitiful me. Isn't that how the song goes? Poor, poor pitiful Carl Heller. Went and messed up. Got a lady killed, he did.

1

Not his fault? There's always a rationalization if you want to use it. But I was rationalizing in the *other* direction. Wallowing in the guilt of it all. And I was coming to think of myself as a first-class creep. What was worse, I was starting to *like* it.

What woke me up was a band of bighorn sheep. At least I happened to be glassing a band of them when it occurred to me for the first time just quite what an ass I was being.

It was late enough in the year that the bighorns were beginning to come down to the valleys, and this bunch was picking its way along behind the lead of an ancient ewe. She was an ugly, patchy-coated old thing, hardly the stuff calendar photos are made of, but she was a wise old thing too, moving with a stately dignity and sureness of direction that could only have come from many seasons of knowledge and experience.

Not far behind her was a half-grown lamb, ewe or ram I couldn't tell, bounding with impatience, springing onto rocks and ledges that the old ewe had disdained, finding dead ends and bounding back to join the flock, dashing to and fro so that it traveled four times as far to accomplish the same amount of descent as the ewe had done so easily.

I watched them in the binoculars and I laughed, and as I did so it occurred to me that that was the first time I had laughed in weeks.

And I wondered briefly which I wanted to be like myself, the old ewe or the busy lamb. I really didn't want an answer but I thought I knew what the answer would be if I permitted myself to give one. I didn't like that.

I turned away from the bighorns and walked back down the slope to the remains of my fire, tossed some wood on the coals to build the flame again, and went to pull the picket pins of my filly and old Belle mare to move them to fresh graze. I wasn't going anywhere in particular, and if I didn't feel like moving camp to another location there was no good reason to do so.

The routines of the camp busywork came automatically, and I found myself taking stock for the first time in quite a while. If I didn't like what I found, that wasn't particularly surprising.

Physically it wasn't so bad, five-foot-eleven and about a

hundred eighty-five pounds, with light brown hair and, now, a whisker growth that was closer to a beard than a stubble. I hadn't shaved since I'd left the ranch in search of . . . What? I had to stop and think about that one.

What had I been searching for out here in the mountains? Peace? I'd been surrounded by peace and tranquility but permitted myself none of it. Joy? I was having none of that either.

Escape, then. But I hadn't escaped from a thing. Hadn't permitted myself even to think about the things that had been bothering me.

I had been burying myself in pity when it wasn't me who deserved pity. Hell, I had no reason to deserve pity. I was alive. I was healthy. I had the capacity to help people instead of hurting them. So what good was I doing out here hiding from everyone? The only person whose opinion counted for anything was myself—my grandfather taught me that long, long ago—and I damn sure couldn't hide from me. I should have proven that to myself weeks ago.

But then, sometimes I am thicker than most.

I sighed and put the coffeepot on the coals, leaned back, and let the crisp, cool air of the high country surround me. A rock formation towered hundreds of feet above my camp. I had been here more than half a day but still hadn't really looked at that ancient, ageless rock. I looked at it now and was able to draw some peace from the grandeur of it.

"Old girl," I said aloud to my elderly mare, "there are times when I envy you your innocence, no decisions and therefore no guilts, just loyalty and a big heart. But I'm wrong every time I do it, because you can't accomplish much either." She raised her head and rolled one large brown eye and flicked an ear in my direction, then went back to her grazing.

"You're right," I said to her. "I don't know what I'm talking about, but at least I'm trying to figure my way through it." I smiled at her. The expression felt odd on my bearded face.

The coffee was boiling. I picked up the pot with one forked stick hooked into the bail and used another to tilt it with the copper loop near the bottom of the pot. The brew smelled good in the cold, high air.

I warmed my hands against my cup and leaned closer to the fire. It was still almighty cold, and finally it occurred to me that it was nearing noon and shouldn't be so cold at this time of day. The sun had been up in a clear sky for hours now.

At least the sky had been clear the last time I looked. It still was, to the east, out toward the plains. That great shoulder of rock was above me to the west, but immediately overhead the sky was beginning to take on the gray, dark look of a midday twilight.

"Girls," I said, "you just might have yourselves a real idiot for a bossman."

I put my coffee down untasted and threw a saddle onto the filly. It would be a ride of at least a mile before I could get up through the notch I remembered seeing north of the camp and get a good look at the weather over that way.

When I did I felt a chill that had nothing to do with the temperature.

The sky to the west was like a solid wall of gunmetal gray, and up here the wind was marching in front of that advancing wall. There was the sharp, ozone taste of snow on that wind, and I knew from experience what would follow it.

If I had been counting the days with any reasonable degree of accuracy, it was early October now. And I had seen the winter storms sweep the high country in September from time to time.

This one that was coming looked like a first-class Bitch of the Back Woods.

And I was at least fifty miles from the nearest shelter that I knew of. More than that from home.

"Young 'un," I said to the filly, "I believe we have found ourselves a problem here."

2

Night came and I hardly noticed the difference. The blowing snow had a luminous quality about it that seemed to take away from the terror of the storm. I could see almost as well in the darkness as I had during the day, although that had been no great shakes to begin with.

The snow was bad and the cold was worse, but what made it dangerous was the wind. The snow and the cold I could cope with well enough. But the wind sent the light, dry, high-country snow swirling and sheeting and building into deep, powdery drifts.

Already, after so few hours, some of those drifts were belly-deep on the horses. Struggling through the drifts sapped their strength at an accelerated rate.

Worse, blowing drifting snow will form cornices and bridges, building ledges of soft powder where the solid earth ends and only empty drops lie below. From horseback—from ski or snowshoe for that matter—it can be impossible to tell where the ground ends and a cornice begins. Ride or walk out onto one and a fall is inevitable.

The drifts can bridge or totally fill crevices that could be easily avoided if they were seen, but in storm conditions that's impossible too.

And blind faith is a poor substitute for good sense in a mountain snowstorm.

The logical and proper thing to do would be for me to hole up and wait out the storm.

Early storms of such ferocity are rarely long-lived. It can happen, of course, but it is rare. Twelve hours, almost certainly no more than twenty-four, and the weather should break again, calm if not quite clear.

I had supplies enough to last me for days if that should

be necessary. A little coffee and a few staples left, a healthy chunk of meat poached far beyond the reach of the game wardens, enough cigarettes to last several days and, more important, probably a half-dozen Bic lighters still in my saddlebags. I could find a hidey-hole in the side of one of the ever-present mountains, a cave or a sheltered spot where I could fashion a windbreak and a reflector for the fire. I would be warm enough and comfortable. When the storm was gone I could walk out at my leisure.

But that was the rub. *Walk* out.

By the time this weather ebbed, the country would be hip-deep on the level, and the drifts would be dozens of feet deep in the hollows.

By the time this storm ended, there would be no way I could hope to get out with the horses.

I could make myself a pair of snowshoes to get my own valued carcass out intact. But how do you fit snowshoes to a horse?

The old Belle mare, rock steady and nerveless on the lead rope behind me, had been with me since I was a kid. The money I had won on that old thing at the open cuttings had gone a long way toward making a man out of me, helping to pay for education both formal and informal. We went through a lot together, that old mare and I. She deserved better than to be abandoned and left to die alone in the snow.

The filly was almost as good a horse. From a technical point of view she showed promise of actually being a better cutting horse when she matured, and if I did not yet have with her the same bond of affection I felt for old Belle, well, it was not her fault. She was an honest thing and a giving one, and she did not deserve a frigid death any more than the old mare did.

What it came down to was that the easy way out for me—holing up and waiting it out—would be simply a matter of buying my comfort with the lives of those two horses.

I could do that. Or I could fight the storm along with them and throw the dice for all three of us.

There didn't seem to be much of a choice to it. I kept on riding into the night.

The country here was not really familiar. It was too far
from the home stamping grounds for me to have used it
frequently, although I had been through a time or two in the
years past. I knew I wasn't going to actually get lost even
if I managed to confuse myself from time to time—and I
am convinced that believing yourself unlosable is one of
the surest guarantees against ever getting lost—and I knew
that if we could only keep at it, eventually we would come
out somewhere in the vicinity of home.

The question was whether we could keep going.

Both horses were caked with a thick rime of frost and
clinging snow. We were quartering into the wind, so their
right sides were coated solid and their right eyes peered
out of crusty white masks whenever one of them looked at
me.

Even so, they looked more comfortable than I felt, and
every few minutes I would pinch myself for assurance that
I still had feeling in my hands and face.

I try to ride out prepared for weather even in the summer.
Hell, I've seen snow on the Fourth of July and in the third
week of August, and I know there are no guarantees I
won't see it between those dates at some time in the
future. I had the usual down vest, which is comfortable the
year around up here, and a down parka. I had the best in
gloves and some space-age thermal liners for my gloves
and socks too. What I had left at home, though, were my
ski masks. Like the old-timers, I was having to resort to
rags—in this case a bath towel—wrapped around my head
with my hat brim pulled down over my ears. I'd have sold
a healthy percentage of my birthright just then for one
woolen ski mask and a pair of goggles.

The beard, by the way, was doing no good at all to
insulate my face from the storm. The wind hit me like the
fur wasn't there, and I began to wonder about the logic of
all the fellows I know in the high country who wear brush
on their faces.

My eyelashes and nose hairs had long since grown spiky
with frost, and I had no idea whether my nose was dry or
drippy.

The filly kept plodding resolutely forward, but her strength
was not what it had been when we broke camp, and the drifts

were getting deeper. Deep enough now that she was having to breast them with a surging, plunging, up-and-down
motion where before she had been able to simply wade
through them like someone trying to run through waist-
deep water. She began to tremble, and I knew it was past
time to switch the chore of breaking trail onto old Belle. I
had been avoiding that, for too long actually, not knowing
whether the old horse was up to the strain. If I killed her
too . . .

I quit that line of thought and pulled up to a halt as soon
as the filly cleared the drift she was fighting. There was no
shelter to get behind here, so the best I could do for them
was to turn their rumps to the wind and give them a few
minutes' rest.

There was nothing here to tie them to and I've never
been one of those fools who trusts a so-called ground
hitch, but these tired girls weren't going anywhere. The
only place the driving wind would have pushed them
would have been back into the drift we had just gotten
through, and they were not likely to try that on their own.
I dropped the reins and lead rope where they were and let
the horses rest.

The visibility was lousy, but I stood with my back to the
force of the wind and looked skyward for a time, hoping to
see a hint of moonlight or *some* damn thing to give me
hope that it was breaking. There was nothing. Which
meant it looked like decision time had arrived.

I still had the option to hole up in comfort. Or to roll
those dice.

Old Belle kind of made the decision for me. She turned
her head and looked at me with that clown mask of snow
and ice her homely old face had become.

The damned old horse had carried me safely through so
much over the years we had been together. She had brought
me in drunk and she had brought me in hurt, and never
once had the old thing failed me.

I went to her and began working at the lashings on her
packsaddle.

Tried to anyway. The nylon cord was frozen into solid
balls at the knots, and my fingers were anything but
nimble anyhow. I struggled with them and cussed them

some until it finally occurred to me how simpleminded I was being about that old habit of preserving a piece of cord. (Have you ever noticed in the movies how the guy just whips out his knife and cuts his own damn catch rope to free a prisoner's tied hands? Drives me nuts. *No*body who uses a rope as part of his livelihood's tools is ever going to do a dumb thing like that.) Well, this was a first for me. I whipped out my knife and cut my own pack lashings.

There was some pretty decent stuff in those packs. An Eddie Bauer sleeping bag and Harley Davidson—don't laugh, it's good gear—cooking equipment and all the food I owned this side of my own comfortable home.

I retrieved my cigarettes and a couple envelopes of dried soup that I shoved into my coat pockets and a tin cup that I tied to my saddle strings. I got a pair of lighters out of the saddlebags and dumped them too. I pitched my canteen and rope off the saddle too. From here on we traveled light and made it or didn't.

The activity should have warmed me, but it didn't. If anything I was feeling colder than before, maybe just from knowing that the decision had been made now and we were going for broke. I switched the saddle from the filly to old Belle and let the packsaddle and blanket fall into the snow.

There is one school of thought, I know, that says a horse will be more comfortable with a blanket and saddle on its back, but I've always held that a range horse— which mine are, winter or summer—is better off naked. I've seen my horses in apparent comfort with ice an inch deep on their backs and the big back-porch thermometer ticking forty below. They couldn't do that, of course, if they were used to barn shelter all the time, but they stay out in the weather regardless. And as far as I'm concerned a blanket in bad weather is only a place to collect sweat and turn it into ice that will reach the skin. Then they will get bad off.

Besides, the filly would get more rest if she didn't have the restrictions of a cinch around her barrel.

So I pitched it all and stepped back onto the old mare that had done so much for me so many times before.

*   *   *

"Dammit!"

I kicked loose of the stirrups and was damned lucky that I got out of them because it had been a long time since I'd felt my feet last. That is one thing about riding through real cold. Your feet aren't flexing like they would be if you were walking or even skiing. They just sit there and get colder.

I hit the soft, cushioning snow and went rolling and windmilling down the slope. The filly was thrashing and sliding a few feet away, and a flailing hoof caught my shoulder a good one as she went. Fortunately my coat and vest gave enough padding that I felt it but wasn't particularly hurt by it.

At least I hoped that was the reason. If I was so cold that I was losing feeling in my trunk, I was already experiencing hypothermia and was well on my way to waking up dead. I wasn't sure actually and might never know since one of the first signs of hypothermia is a loss of judgment ability. The brain functions slow, and how do you judge for yourself if that is happening?

We reached the bottom of the slope at about the same time, and the filly was mired in the clinging softness of yet another drift. She was on her back with her legs waving in the air, and I had to get to her quick before she panicked or twisted a gut or something.

Belle, that wise old thing, was picking her way down the slope above us one step at a time. She didn't seem to need any help.

I tried to pull the filly over, but the drift was too deep so I had to get down and use my arms to scoop snow out from under her side until I could roll her over into the depression and eventually get her back onto her feet.

It worked, but I was one winded SOB before I was done.

The movement made me feel a bit warmer anyhow, and after a while I realized that at last my growth of beard was doing some good. A crust of ice had formed on it from my breathing—didn't want to quit that—and seemed to be trapping some body heat against my face. My ears were gone but all in all I wasn't in as bad shape as I might have been. Something to be thankful about for sure.

"I think, girls," I told them, "that we could do for some shelter." My voice sounded odd, and I realized that I was talking like a gangster in a fifties B movie. Not moving my lips. It hurt when I tried to move them.

I got back onto the filly—I suppose I should have switched the saddle again but I wasn't sure that my fingers were up to the job—and blundered on until I found a grove of spruce in which to hide from the wind.

I tied the horses to a branch and crawled under an overhang of branches and living needles to reach some semblance of a shelter. Dead or at least dry lower limbs gave me the makings for a fire, and after half a dozen two-handed attempts I got some flame going. Opened my coat to that sucker and just basked in the warmth.

It made all the difference.

After a few minutes—I knew better than to lie down and try to take it easy for even the briefest amount of time—I killed the fire and went back to the horses before they could stiffen up and realize how cold and miserable they must be.

I was able to make the saddle switch this time. When I realized that I could actually see what I was doing, I figured dawn must have come. I hadn't hardly noticed it before.

About eight the wind slacked off, and I realized that sometime during the past hour or three it had quit snowing too. The wind had been blowing the previously fallen stuff so much that I hadn't seen any difference.

I stopped Belle on a rise and listened. Somewhere off in front of us I could hear the clatter and growl of a snow-plow at work, and I knew we couldn't be too awfully far from U.S. 24.

I looked around to a white but familiar skyline and began to grin. We had come out—almost out, anyhow—near Wilkerson Pass and not too terribly far from Lake George. Somehow during the night we must have crossed the Tarryall road without me ever seeing it, because we were sure on the wrong side of it now.

I switched my saddle back to the filly for the last leg home and headed out again.

I don't even know why I did it, but when I got to Lake George a couple hours later it never even occurred to me that I could have stopped there for coffee and warmth and human conversation. Even for a ride home and some borrowed feed and shelter for the horses. I just rode on through with my head down toward my chest and took the road for the home place.

Sillier still, once I finally made it home and pulled up by the door, I just sat there with the reins in my hands and a fresh fall of snow piling up on the back of my neck. I didn't care a thing about getting off the filly or going inside. I was home and that seemed to be enough, so I just sat where I was and let the sleep come over me.

3

"Carl? Carl! Damn you, man, help me here."

I smiled at him. It was my neighbor—friend too—Walter from down the road. I sort of remembered passing his place on the way home. That seemed like it had been a long time ago.

"Come on, dammit. Turn loose of those reins." He was beside me, standing on the ground. His turbo diesel Scout was nearby, but I hadn't heard him drive up. I wondered how he could have done that without me hearing him coming. A good trick, I thought. Nicely done.

The filly sidestepped, and I shifted my weight automatically to go with her motion.

"Come on, Carl, loosen up there." Walter was prying at my fingers. He pulled the reins out of them and they fell, the reins and my clenched hands too.

Walter came around to the right side of the horse and I could feel him pulling my foot out of the stirrup there; then he came back around to the left side and did the same thing. I smiled at him again. Good man, Walter.

"You have to help me, Carl."

I would have, but I didn't know what he wanted.

Walter is none too young and none too brawny, so he got me down in the most logical way possible. He gave a yank on my arm, and I wasn't horseback anymore.

"Help me, Carl. Push. That's it, push."

Somehow the old rascal got me inside, though I still don't see how he got it done. He weighs a good fifty pounds less than I do and is somewhere in his seventies, old enough to be twice retired. But he did it.

He draped me onto the sofa, more or less, and I gave him another neighborly smile. I was feeling real good, actually. Very friendly with the whole world. Then I remembered.

"The horses," I told him. It sounded like a croak rather than a pair of words even to me, and I knew what I was trying to say, but he seemed to understand it all right.

"I will," he said. "In just a minute."

He disappeared from sight, and I didn't have the will to turn my head and see where he had gone. After a moment I heard bathwater running, and I hoped he was running it for me. A bath sounded pretty nice. It had been weeks since I'd had a proper washing. I got to wondering if my body odor was offensive and worried about that while Walter came back and stripped me naked.

Once again we went through the push-and-carry routine, ending up this time with the valued Heller self nearly submerged in a tub of cold water. I could tell from the feel of the water at my crotch and lower belly that the water was cold, but everywhere else it felt quite warm. I was trying to sort that out when Walter said, "Don't slide down and drown now, you idiot. I'm going to get a fire started and put the horses up. Then I'll come back and run some warmer water for you."

I nodded, or tried to. I was perfectly content with whatever Walter wanted to do. Except that a prickly, pins-and-needles sensation was beginning to make me itch. I wished he would make that go away.

In what seemed only two and a half seconds or thereabouts, Walter was back.

"I took the horses out to the barn," he was saying. "I rubbed them down and gave them some hay and a little grain. They were more thirsty than hungry, I think. And I have a fire going in the living room, and the coffee is almost ready. How are you feeling?"

I smiled at him.

Walter shook his head and rubbed at the back of his neck. "This is all my own fault, I suppose, for having a fool for a neighbor." He bent down to run some warm water into the tub and began rubbing at my feet and hands.

Later, much later, he wrapped me in a huge terrycloth towel and helped me out to the living room. I was feeling close to human by then. Hot coffee and a tot of homemade, double-run, sour-mash, white whiskey completed the job he had started.

The fire felt damn good. Like most up here I do my heating with wood, although I have a propane furnace that I can leave with the thermostat turned low when I'm going to be away. Generally speaking it is preferable to come home to a house where the pipes are not frozen. No furnace can compete with a fire in a cast-iron stove, though, for the kind of heat that will reach the bones. I huddled close to it and took another drink first of the whiskey and then of the coffee.

"You look better," Walter observed.

"Feel better too, thanks to you. Good grief, man, you don't suppose I'm actually going to have to *thank* you, do you?"

"You came close to it," he said.

"Listen . . ." I was still weak and was feeling a bit choked up or something.

"Shut up before you ruin this for me," he ordered. "I'm enjoying a period of gloating and smug superiority now. I would rather you didn't disturb that."

"Yessir."

Walter shook his head. "You were in rough shape, Carl. Didn't you realize the temperature has been dropping steadily since dawn?"

I shook my head. It was the truth. Aside from the obvious fact that I wasn't carrying a thermometer, by dawn I'd been so numbed to the cold that I was a long way past being able to distinguish any changes in the temperature.

"Well, it has been. That was one blue whistler of a storm, but it didn't really start to get cold until the sky cleared. How far back were you?"

"I don't know. Fifty, sixty miles maybe."

"You were lucky."

"I can't argue with you. Especially after I got here. I don't know what happened. I let down when I reached the gate, I guess. All the fight was used up or something."

"When I saw you ride past I wasn't even sure it was you. You and the horses were just so many white shapes. But I realized no one else would be foolish enough to be out in this weather. Where is your gear?"

"To tell you the truth, Walter, I don't really know. The visibility was so bad I'm not sure where I dumped it. Come a good thaw and a reasonable long-range weather forecast, I can go out looking for it. It will keep until then. And if somebody else finds it first, well, I can't do much complaining about the loss. The horses never would have made it through carrying all that junk." I sighed. "So how have things been around here?"

Walter chuckled. "Behind you and forgotten, is it?"

"Why not."

"True." He grinned. "They are talking about another electric rate increase."

"Walter old friend, you sure know how to make a fellow feel like he's back to civilization."

"Isn't that the truth. Other than that, though, everything is fine. I put some hay out for your horses yesterday when I heard the weather reports, and I got your heater out and put it in the stock tank. You really should clean that thing someday, you know."

"Yes sir, I am really and truly home if you are going to start nagging at me about such trivia."

"Oh, and you had a visitor. About a week and a half ago. Something like that. He said his name was, um . . ." Walter dug into his hip pocket and pulled out his wallet and a scrap of paper where he had written down the name. "Glen Goodroe, that was it. He acted like he was in a serious hurry to see you. He was quite disappointed when I told him where you were and that you couldn't be reached until you decided to come home."

I thought for a moment. "The name rings bells back there somewhere, but it's been a while. Hey, I remember now. I'll bet he's just wanting permission to hunt the place at the last minute."

I remembered him now, more or less. He used to be a friend, or at least a fairly close acquaintance, of my father's. Goodroe came out to the ranch several times with hunting parties. As best I could recall, he had been a passable shot and easy enough to get along with, no bad habits like doing his hunting with a bottle instead of a gun. And he had been partial to gadgets. That was probably why I could remember him after all this time while I would have forgotten most of the men my dad dragged out here from time to time. Goodroe liked his toys, things like range finders back when they were rare and a pair of binoculars with a camera built into them. I had been impressed. Which meant that I sure must have been young at the time. I don't think I had heard his name mentioned since then.

"I don't believe he was looking for a place to hunt," Walter said. "He acted too serious for that."

"There are some folks," I told him, "who get real serious about their hunting."

"And every one of them has a thousand square miles of public land to do it on within a day's drive from home," he reminded me. "I got the impression it might be something . . . business-related. Your kind of business, Carl."

Well, I value Walter's judgment, and with good reason. And while I don't talk about my sideline—I wouldn't exactly call it a regular form of work—with just anyone, Walter knows more about it than just about anybody else ever will.

What it is, I do a favor occasionally and maybe pick up a dollar or two in the process.

Once upon a time, long long ago as the saying goes, I was young and innocent and a law student. I was idealistic enough to believe then that that was a way a person could help other people by seeing that justice was done.

But that isn't the way things work in the real world. I found out soon enough that the law is one thing and justice is another. The two are entirely unrelated.

Personally I was always taught that justice is the desirable thing. Then I learned the hard way that the law has no more interest in actual justice than your average hog does. It was disillusioning at the time.

I dropped out of law school and played some on the rodeo circuit; then my grandfather died and left me the family ranch up here. I settled in to raise registered Quarter Horses and Texas longhorn cattle, but after a while, one way or another, I found myself taking on these little favors for friends. Mostly when they got themselves into problems where the law wouldn't help them find justice. Like I said, I got myself disillusioned with the one but not with the other.

Since then there have been some who have called me a sort of one-man vigilante committee, although that is a description I am not particularly in favor of. Vigilance committees had a nasty habit of getting out of hand within about two minutes of having served their purpose back in the old days. That is a thing I hope I won't be guilty of myself and something I have to guard against.

On the other hand, an awful lot of liberal professorial types nowadays will condemn the old-time vigilance committees for all the bad they did but fail to remember that there once was a good and a necessary side to them too.

So I try to keep my attention on the justice part of it and watch out for the personal-vendetta stuff.

It really isn't so much of a juggling act as long as a fellow doesn't take himself too seriously.

"Are you feeling any better now than when you left, Carl?"

I looked down at my wrinkled, robe-swathed body and gave him a grin.

"I don't mean physically. When you rode out of here you acted like you didn't care if you came back or not."

"I don't know, Walter. I guess I was pretty low. Now . . ." I shrugged. "You can't accomplish much by quitting."

"Do you want to talk about it?"

I shook my head. I can tell Walter very nearly anything. Certainly he doesn't repeat any of what he hears. But the key word there is "nearly." And it was too long a story to want to go into anyway.

Walter, bless him, accepted that without argument. He got up and poured refills.

We sat for a while in silence, which is one of the advantages of a good friendship. You don't have to work at filling every quiet period that comes along. After a few minutes Walter said, "Whatever it was, Carl, it isn't out of your system yet."

"That's the natural truth." I took another swallow of the warming liquor.

"I think," he said, "if you mope around here by your-self any longer, you're going to do nothing but worry about things that are over and done with. I think you need some involvement, Carl. You need to get out and see other people, try to do some good for someone or something outside your own problems. I think you need something like that right now.''

I shrugged again. But the truth was that he was probably right. I'd spent more than enough time already being self-indulgent.

"You know it's no big thing for me to keep an eye on your place awhile longer," he said.

That was true enough, too. One of the advantages to raising livestock the old-fashioned way is that the critters are expected to watch out for themselves. Horses and cattle both, I turn them out on more than enough graze and let them go about their business. During the winter when there is no gathering or training to be done, the only choring necessary around my place is to make sure the water tank is relatively free of ice. Walter doesn't mind doing that for me when I'm gone, any more than I mind returning the favor when he wants to go somewhere. Between us we get along pretty well that way.

"What I think you should do," Walter went on, "is go talk to this Goodroe. If he only wants a place to hunt, you haven't lost anything. If he has a problem you could help with, well, the benefit might be more yours than his.''

"I'll think about it."

He took a deep swallow from his glass and all of a sudden this look of sheer horror came over his craggy face. I thought he was having some sort of attack—Walter isn't, after all, a young man by any stretch of the imagination—and was halfway out of my chair.

"Damn," he blurted. "I left a pot of beans on the stove." He bolted out the door without another word, and a moment later I heard his Scout roaring away with a loud, diesel clatter. I didn't hear any sirens from the volunteer fire department so after a while I figured he must still have a house. I tottered up onto my own two legs and went to bed. It had been a rather long night.

4

Someone picked up on the other end after the third ring. "Goodroe residence." It was a woman's voice with no intonations to say whether it was Mrs. Goodroe or a maid.

"I'm trying to reach Glen Goodroe, ma'am. I looked in the Yellow Pages but there doesn't seem to be a listing for Goodroe Business Equipment." The name of the man's business had come to me as I was driving down Ute Pass in the Jeep. The last I knew, Goodroe had been running a fairly large business-equipment dealership—office furniture, typewriters, calculators, and all that—in Colorado Springs.

I could have tried calling ahead, I suppose, but it isn't much of a drive from Lake George down onto the flatlands, and there was some shopping I wanted to do. I was also discovering that the thought of being away from home and among strangers was not altogether unpleasant for a change. So maybe I was more ready than I'd given myself credit for for quitting my moping and getting back to the real world.

"Mr. Goodroe can be reached at G&G Electronics," the voice informed me.

"Thank you, ma'am." I hung up and checked the phone book again. The listing was there, along with an address on the north end of town.

It was a fine day, warm almost to the point of being hot now that the cold front had passed through on its way to Kansas and Iowa and points east, and I had the soft top of the CJ7 folded down. I decided I would rather drive over to G&G Electronics than call.

I was expecting a store of some sort, perhaps dealing in computers or electronic calculators or even the newfangled typewriters, again under a different business name. What I

20

found instead was a small, very modern and very sterile-looking building made of pale gray brick, windowless and no doubt very efficient. It looked new. It also was quite obvious that G&G Electronics was not in any retail business dealing directly with the buying public. The firm's name was on an inconspicuous little metal sign set on the lawn in front of the place, and if I had not been watching the street numbers closely I never would have spotted it.

The parking lot was small too and was nearly filled by the seven or eight cars parked there behind the building. No formalities like reserved slots for bosses or visitors I noticed as I wheeled the Jeep into the open spot nearest the entrance.

I wondered briefly about leaving my bags untended with the top down. That is something I never have to think about at home. In fact, my car keys won't leave the ignition from one city visit to the next. Down in the Springs that can be a foolhardy habit. I decided not to worry about it, though. Once you start fretting about the improbable, it is hard to know when to stop.

The inside of G&G was chilly and there was a curiously sterile smell to the air. But the receptionist was pretty. She reminded me of WKRP's Jennifer if a bit less buxom. She was also wearing a wedding ring. Lucky fella, whoever he was.

"Yes, sir?" She sounded eager to please despite my scruffy appearance.

At least I was still regarding myself as having a scruffy look about me. I had spent some time peering into the mirror that morning and decided to let the well-started beard remain for a little while to see if I liked it. The book was still out on that, but she would have no way of knowing that I hadn't gone around with fur on my face for the past dozen years or so.

"Mr. Goodroe, please."

"Might I ask which Mr. Goodroe?"

"Glen." I hadn't known there was more than one. Glen was the only one I remembered from those long-past hunts.

The girl smiled very attractively. "And could I ask which Mr. Glen Goodroe, sir?"

"You really do give a fella a choice, don't you?"

"We try, sir. In this instance, the choices are Senior or Junior."

"The gentleman I'm looking for would be, oh, fiftyish, maybe sixty."

"That would be Mr. Goodroe Senior, sir." She reached for her telephone. "Do you have an appointment, Mr. . . .?"

"Heller. Carl Heller. And I'm just dropping by. No appointment."

"Yes, sir." She pushed a button, and I could hear a telephone buzz somewhere not too far away in the place. The buzzing quit and she passed the message along. "Mr. Goodroe's office is right through that door, sir. First door on your left." She was smiling so nicely that I had to return it in kind.

Goodroe met me at the door of his office with a handshake and a hearty welcome. He ushered me inside like it was old-home week, saying how delighted he was to see me so unexpectedly after so long and how much he had liked my father and how much he regretted Dad's passing and all that. At least he did sound genuinely sincere about that and did not try to make the relationship out to have been more than it really was. I liked that about him.

The man had not changed much from the way I remembered him. Much more gray in his hair now, but still tall and looking tanned and fit, the kind of healthy appearance that comes from regular workouts with a racket and a sun lamp. He had a look about him, too, that said those workouts would be taken at a private club and not at the Y. The scent of an expensive cologne preceded him by at least two feet when he moved.

"This is such a surprise," he said several times. Pointedly, I thought. There was no mention of the fact that he had been up at the ranch looking for me. Without thinking about it, I followed his lead and neglected to bring that up myself.

"Tell me about yourself, Carl. Surely you aren't still rodeoing for a living."

"No, I raise a few horses and a few head of cattle," I said. "I do a little of this and that to stay busy."

"Well, that's fine. Is the hunting still good up your way?"

"Not bad. I don't like to harvest much of the game I have up there." I wondered if Walter had been wrong for a change and we were now about to get to the real reason he had wanted to see me.

"Any bear?"

"A few. I leave them alone, though. There aren't many, and they aren't the stock killers most people seem to believe." If the man wanted to come and shoot one of my blackies, he was going to be disappointed. A black bear is a lot more interesting to watch than to kill, and until or unless they went after my calves, I would probably leave them be.

Goodroe nodded. "Warren Prew and I hunted bear together in the San Juans this season. You know Warren, don't you?"

I nodded.

"He brought home an outstanding boar, and I got a nice little two-hundred-pounder. It was a good hunt. We got to talking about the hunts we had had with your father. He and Warren used to go out together often, I understand. I believe Warren mentioned then that you were on the ranch permanently now."

Warren had been one of my father's closest friends, and he made a point of keeping in touch with me now that Dad was gone. I liked him when I was a kid, and I still do.

"Say, Carl, would you like to take a tour of this old mill?"

It wasn't what I'd had in mind exactly, but I couldn't see any way to say no without offending the man. I told him I'd just purely love nothing better, or something to that effect.

Actually it turned out to be right interesting.

Goodroe had always been into gadgets, as I already remembered and he admitted as well, and when downsized computers became so popular he was right in there with his fascination.

It started as a deductible aid to his business, quickly became a hobby, and then, when he discovered an aptitude

for such things, led him to sell out his business-equipment
store and launch G&G Electronics.

So far they were into software programming, writing
and copyrighting and selling computer programs to be used
in other people's hardware for this business purpose or
that. I didn't begin to understand the exact functions he
was telling me about, but it seemed they had seven programs they were now peddling in a highly competitive
market and were doing pretty well with them. Most of the
G&G shop was devoted to producing preprogrammed tapes
and disks compatible with state-of-the-industry hardware.

"That is our bread and butter, Carl. Over here in our
research-and-development wing"—he laughed when he said
it, and a moment later I understood why, when he opened
the door it was onto a very small room—"is our aspiration
department."

As far as I could tell from looking at what I was seeing
there, it might well have been what you would get if you
turned a bright junior-high-school student loose in a Heathkit
warehouse or gave him unlimited funds and a Radio Shack
catalog. It was bits and pieces of hardware, but beyond
that I was lost.

"I'm a frustrated inventor, Carl. I like to invent gadgets
as well as play with them. This one, if it works out the
way I intend, could be the end of the rainbow. As a matter
of fact, I'm naming it the Rainbow Drive."

"Oh, really?" I hoped I sounded interested. Goodroe
was obviously as proud as a new pappy with his intended
invention.

"You've heard of the Winchester Drive system, of
course."

I hadn't, but it didn't seem sociable to argue the point.

"The Rainbow Drive will have the advantages of the
same extremely large byte-storage capability as the Winchester, plus it will be readily adaptable to existing small
office hardware. RAM, of course, and an extraordinarily
rapid drive. The advantages are obvious."

Obvious, I thought. I didn't know what the hell he was
talking about. But then, if I started spouting resins or
rearsets at Glen Goodroe, he wouldn't know what I was

saying either. Every limited interest has its own jargon. His just didn't happen to be mine.

"As soon as the Rainbow development is completed and the patents applied for, we will have to expand. We've been here just at two years now, but we wouldn't begin to have enough floor space once we are ready to gear up for the Rainbow Drive. We'll . . . Say, Carl, I'll bet you would like to see our expansion site." He laughed. "Actually, I would like you to see it. At the moment there is no plant there and I have some horses on it that I bought for my little girl. I spent a bundle on those animals because she thought they were pretty, and I haven't the faintest idea if I was taken or not. Perhaps you could tell me."

Perhaps you might not want to know, I thought to myself. Someone who doesn't know bloodlines and conformation might as well wear a tag reading "Sucker" when he goes horse shopping for daddy's little girl.

But what I said was that I'd be enormously enchanted by the very idea. Mm, maybe not quite that thick, but almost.

Goodroe bustled me back to his office to get his jacket and then herded me out the door. "Would you mind driving, Carl? It isn't far."

"Not if you don't mind getting windblown. I have the top down today."

"That sounds wonderful," he said with an air of vast cheerfulness. "I haven't ridden in a convertible in ages."

I led the way out to my Jeep, let him get settled, and then pulled out of the lot and into traffic.

We had gone perhaps a quarter-mile when I glanced over at my passenger.

Glen Goodroe was slumped in the seat looking haggard and ten years older than he had seemed back at the plant. "Are you all right?"

He shook his head. The man looked utterly miserable.

5

I began to pull over to the side, but Goodroe motioned me on. "Please. I said we were going over to the new site. We need to go there."

It was all right by me. He gave directions, and in a few minutes we were there. It was a piece of very pretty gently rolling land north of town, up on a hillside with a view of the Front Range Mountains and of the Air Force Academy. From the gate you could see, very small in the distance, the distinctive shape of the Academy's famous chapel.

"Very nice," I said. I didn't really know what else *to* say. Goodroe still looked awful.

"I'm sorry, Carl."

I raised my eyebrows a notch.

"That act I had to put on back there." He shook his head. "You don't know what it has been like."

"Obviously I don't," I agreed.

He sighed. It was a long and a very unhappy sound. "I never know when someone might be listening. That was why I wanted to come in your car."

"Bugs?" I asked.

He nodded. "Listening devices. Eavesdroppers. I really don't know what might be involved."

"Maybe you should tell me about it."

Again that tired, empty sigh. "I have had, well, several professional detection firms come in. They used electronic countermeasures and sweepers. They found nothing. Nothing at all. But I *know* . . ." He slumped even lower in the bucket seat. "The last firm suggested that I might be experiencing a form of paranoia, Carl. I am *not*." The poor man sounded more defensive than certain of that.

"I know industrial espionage is a fact of life these days,

Glen, but why you in particular? And how do you know it's happening?"

"The Rainbow Drive would have to be the reason for it. I was serious when I said that that drive would be a major improvement. It will make someone a great deal of money. A great deal," he repeated.

I figured I could safely take his word for that. From the little I've read about the computer industry, it is already huge and growing steadily huger in great gulps. If this or any other invention was likely to capture a large share of that market, the profit potential would be enormous.

And of course wherever there is big money available there are always people around willing to take big risks to siphon off a piece of it. Still . . .

"As for why I think my plant has been penetrated, Carl, one of the very early improvements I made, a minor but very necessary mechanical change from the production norm, has already been patented by one of my competitors."

"But couldn't that have been simply a coincidence, Glen? I understand the automobile was 'invented' by three different people, in three different countries, at almost the exact same time. Things like that happen."

"Of course they do. That is what one of those surveillance firms told me too, Carl. So I checked the Patent Office drawings." He looked at me. "Carl, they hadn't even bothered to copy those drawings. They were mine, right down to a misstroke of the pen along one edge. They were *my* drawings, and now the patent has been granted to someone else."

Goodroe gave me a tight, grim smile. "They won't stop me that way. They made me back up and find an alternative, but I think I have it and it will be better than either the original or the new patent. But if I can't stop this thing . . ." He looked haggard.

"I don't know where to turn, Carl. The professionals in this field, well, they've turned out to be no help at all. They think I am a paranoid old man with imaginary fears to blame for future failures. All of their gadgets turned up nothing, so they concluded that there was nothing to find."

"I don't know a thing about gadgets, Glen," I told him honestly enough. "I wouldn't know a toaster from a vacuum cleaner if somebody put slots in the top of the vacuum.''

Again there was that grim smile. ''Maybe what I need, Carl, is a man with some common sense and more than his share of good luck. I . . . understand you have a certain instinct for this sort of thing.''

That surprised me. I don't exactly advertise my sideline.

''You remember I told you I was hunting with Warren this year?''

I nodded.

''A man's conversations can wander in strange directions over a campfire. Warren doesn't know anything about my particular problem, but one night we were discussing your dad, and Warren was telling me about one of the last times they were out together.''

''That would have been for sheep up in Alaska?'' It was, bluntly, a test question. I remembered good and well the last time my father and Warren Prew had hunted.

''It was for sheep, but I thought Warren said they were in British Columbia.'' I shrugged it off as if it were unimportant, but they had flown to B.C. for the hunt.

''Anyway,'' Glen went on, ''Warren was saying that your dad had been bragging on you. He was quite proud of some things you had done, even though he was still upset about your leaving law school.''

Proud of me? My father? That was . . . a surprise. So much so that I wasn't quite sure how to handle it. If he ever felt anything approaching pride after I quit school and went ''on the bum'' as he insisted it was, he damn sure never gave any hint of it to me.

Disappointment, if anything. Anger, sure. Fury, even. But pride? That was something he had never expressed to me in word or action, either one. I wondered if it could be so. I *wanted* it to be, but I was skeptical too. It was so foreign to everything that had been between us those last few years. I wondered.

''He told Warren about several, um, adventures you had gotten into,'' Goodroe was saying. I tried to pay attention. ''And Warren told me about them. The way I understand it, you try to help people when the law can or will not. Is that correct?''

"More or less," I answered without much interest. Frankly, I was thinking about other things just then.

"Whatever your fee is, Carl, I will pay it. I need help. I don't know where else to turn."

I tried to put my thoughts back on business. "I don't exactly have a fee schedule, Glen. I'm not licensed and there's nothing formal about what I do. I just try to mix in and help where I can. If I don't do any good for someone, we shake hands and forget it ever happened. If I do, well, I'm not always in a position to know how much help I've been. I let the other party determine that and pass along whatever seems reasonable."

Goodroe nodded. "Carl, I would really appreciate it if you would—how did you put it?—mix in around my plant. I know there is a leak there somewhere. The future well-being of my entire family depends on finding and stopping that situation. It is really important to me. And to my children."

"I can't make you any promises, Glen. You have to understand that up front."

"I am not asking for promises. Just for a look." He paused. "My drive could be worth millions of dollars, Carl. Literally millions."

I whistled. To me the concept of a million is just a bunch of zeros written down on paper. To Goodroe it was something that could be just around the corner.

"If you are successful," Goodroe said, "your fee would be commensurate."

I will admit that that tickled my attention some. There are some people who claim that cash is nasty stuff and they have no interest in it. Personally, I make it a point to distrust anyone I hear saying that. I like the stuff right well myself.

I reached across to shake hands. "I guess I'll give it a whirl, Glen."

The poor bastard smiled. He might have been a whole lot happier in the long run if I had gone back home right then, but he smiled and shook my hand and we had a deal of sorts.

*   *   *

Goodroe insisted that we go through the motions of looking over the expansion site as had been announced back at the plant.

He had sixty acres there, and we walked the land together, Goodroe pointing out how the building would be situated and where this or that would be. There were some surveyors' stakes in the ground, so at least the preliminary drawings had been done and work was ready to begin as soon as Goodroe had reason to start it. That would depend on the successful development of his pot of gold at the end of the Rainbow.

In the meantime the grassy land was being used as pasture for a pair of extremely well-built geldings. I was more interested in seeing them than the land, actually. When I asked Glen about their bloodlines, he laughed.

"I know less about horses than you do about electronics, Carl. Sandy could tell you all that, but all I know about them is the size of the check that was written." He mentioned the figure, which was enough to make me whistle. He patted the muzzle of a blood bay that had come over to us in search of a handout. "This one is supposed to be some kind of champion, and the red horse"—he pointed toward the sorrel nearby—"is some other kind of high muckamuck. I can't tell them apart except by color."

"I can't tell you if you were taken or not, actually, but both of them are built right."

"Ask Sandy if you want to know anything about them."

"Sandy is your little girl?"

"Yes. She's a peach. Very much her mother's daughter."

"I'll ask her, then."

We turned away and went back to the Jeep. I hooked the wire gap behind us, and Goodroe said, "One thing more, Carl. If you won't accept a regular fee, perhaps you would be able to stay with us while you are here. We have a guest room. And I wouldn't feel right about asking you to incur expenses."

I thought about that for a moment. Normally I'm not much for houseguesting among strangers. But right now I was feeling a need for human company. I thought about it and I said that I would. He seemed to be genuinely pleased by that answer.

"I feel much better already, Carl."

"Please don't, Glen. Wait and see if I can help you. If I do, well, that would be the time to feel better about it. Until then I'm just a visitor. Okay?"

"All right." He smiled. It was the first really pleasant smile I had seen on his face. "But I do feel better, like it or not."

I hoped I wasn't going to disappoint the man. He seemed to be all right for a city fellow.

6

"I hope you don't mind," Goodroe said. We were back in the office, and he was acting as if our conversation had never taken place out at the expansion site. "I have a little business get-together scheduled tonight, but of course you should join us. Junior and Sandy will meet us there, and you and I can pick up the clients. He operates a small chain of computer specialty stores in Chicago."

"I don't know, Glen, I . . ."

"It isn't anything heavy. Far from it." He grinned. "As a matter of fact, I'm betting you'll have a good time."

That I doubted. Business dinners. The idea conjured up visions of a bunch of lecherous old drunks, the out-of-towners expecting a little hired "entertainment" afterward and the locals expecting to provide it. That wasn't my idea of a high old time. Prudish? I don't think so. Selective, yes, and generally sober except when among people I truly like.

But it looked like I was trapped. "Whatever you say, then."

When Goodroe was done in the office we moved my stuff from the Jeep to the trunk of his Caddy, and I dragged a sport coat out to improve the flavor of my appearance. I hadn't brought a suit along—hardly ever wear one—and if he wanted more than that I would cheerfully withdraw from the festivities.

As it happened, he didn't mention it.

The prospects turned out to be a middle-aged man and his wife. They were from Chicago, but they acted like nice folks in spite of that handicap. Goodroe introduced them as Bernie and Irene Noble. Me he introduced just as an old family friend from 'way back in the mountains, which se

32

Mrs. Noble off on a long discussion of minerals and gemstones. It seemed she was a rockhound.

"Yes, ma'am." I'll bet I said that phrase two thousand, four hundred and twenty-nine times, more or less, on the way up Ute Pass.

We turned off at the Pikes Peak toll road exit and came to a stop almost immediately, in front of a pale stucco building that I'm sure I've seen hundreds of times without ever once noticing it in particular. The big sign said it was a cabaret, and I stifled a groan.

A tall, silver-haired Kenny Rogers lookalike greeted Goodroe by name, and we drifted back into a small, busy bar.

There I began to pay some attention to what was going on around me.

I don't mean to imply that the Nobles were not nice people, far from it, but Mrs. Noble couldn't begin to compare with the exquisite nymph who rose out of the crowd with a smile when Glen Goodroe entered the room.

She was . . . breathtaking, the way a horn in the belly is breathtaking, right now and all the way. And I couldn't for the life of me figure out how or why.

Medium height. Medium build. Medium-brown shade of medium-length hair. Nicely formed, but on close analysis, quite ordinary—medium, you might say—features. The only thing really extraordinary about her was her eyes, which were simply huge and a pale green-flecked gray and looked like they had no end to the depth of them.

Yet all of those mediums put together made up a whole that was as stunningly lovely a young woman as I have seen in . . . Since I can remember. That's all. She was, plain and simple, something special—out-of-the-ordinary indeed. Enough to make a fellow pant and paw the ground. I guessed her age to be in the very early twenties, and I had the ugly, fleeting question in my mind about whether a girl like this could be part of some businessman's hired entertainment. If that was so, I decided, it would be one of the most deplorable wastes I had yet seen.

The young man who had stood with her I paid less attention to, for obvious reasons. Only enough to observe that he was young and a hair on the pudgy side. Perhaps more soft and unformed than pudgy, really, and that he looked like he should be wearing jeans and sneakers and carrying some textbooks instead of standing here in blue-serge finery. That quick impression and then back to the girl.

"Sandy, Junior," Goodroe was saying, "I'd like you to meet . . ."

That was as far as I was listening. This incredible creature was Glen Goodroe's "little girl" of the expensive geldings and the photo on his desk showing her with short hair and braces. I couldn't see that kid anywhere in this lithesome creature.

I found myself standing there wringing the brim of my Stetson in my hands and wearing an inane toothy grin. I got to hoping I didn't have any tobacco stuck to my teeth. Then I realized just how juvenile I was being. Made me feel like a bit of an ass, really.

"Carl will be staying with us for a few days," Goodroe was saying. That announcement was met with polite disinterest by all hands.

We settled at a table, and Goodroe ordered a round of drinks. The grown-ups—I couldn't help thinking of them that way—had a normal assortment of mixed drinks, while I was the Lone Stranger swilling Coors. Sandy asked for a Smith and Curry, which seemed to be a specialty of the place, and Junior went on at some length describing the precise concoction he required. It was some kind of phenomenally complicated thing, the name of which I immediately rejected from memory, and he specified each and every brand for each and every part of the combination. By the time all that crap was put into one pot there would be no way to tell the difference, of course, but he had to have it just so.

Goodroe and the Nobles got into a discussion that I couldn't begin to follow, jargon obviously having to do with computers, although beyond that I cannot declaim. The only part I could decipher had to do with the kinds of figures that have dollar signs in front of them. They were talking about orders in the hundreds of thousands of dollars. That much I could fathom.

And this, I kept reminding myself, was concerning the already existing software part of the business. The penny-

ante side of it. If Goodroe's Rainbow Drive invention was
going to make this sound like peanuts, it was going to be
something to behold. No wonder the man was so anxious
about it.

While I was trying to keep half of an ear politely on that
part of the conversation, just in case Mrs. Noble started
asking rockhound questions again, Junior sat in a not
particularly pleasant silence, hunched over his glass with a
straw linking it to his face. The few times he looked
toward his father it was with a grimace.

Which left me with the girl.

It was a social obligation, of course, and I accepted the
task with manful fortitude.

"Your dad showed me your horses today," I ventured.

That brought a smile. "The horses, or the plant
expansion?"

"Well . . ."

"They aren't bad fellas."

"Quarters?"

"Yes." She was more animated now, and it took practically no persuasion to convince her I was interested. I
didn't say in what, but I do also like horses.

The bay was Skipper W blood, by way of Lad's Image
and Lad's Flaming Image, and was an AQHA champion
with most of the points coming in English riding events
like hunt seat and jumping. The sorrel had Impressive
Image blood and was a Superior in trail riding. Sandy
Goodroe was also something of an impressive image, and I
enjoyed hearing every word of it.

Junior, I noticed, was even less interested in the horses
than his father was. I didn't mind that a bit, since it
allowed me to monopolize the girl's conversation.

Dinner was excellent, hosted by the same Kenny Rogers
lookalike, whose name turned out to be, disappointingly,
Bob. He was also the owner, the cook, and the playwright/
producer of the melodrama that followed the meal.

In theory, melodramas are hokey, touristy stuff that no
self-respecting mountain boy should want to have anything
to do with. In practice I was having a helluva good time,
booing the villain and groaning loudly when the ingenue

was endangered and cheering with gusto whenever the hero walked onstage. It was fun, by damn. Surprised me, it did.

Afterward we joined the flow out of the theater area and back to the bar.

There was a little dancing going on, and the melodrama actors and actresses—the same people who had been waiting table a little while before, I finally realized—were gathered around a piano having a singalong with the guests. The Nobles went to fetch a round of drinks and got sidetracked into the piano-side crowd.

"While we have a moment," Goodroe said, "I want to explain why Carl will be visiting with us. He's going to help us find our leak in the business. That is why he is here. Junior, I want you to give him any help he needs at the plant. Anything at all. We have no secrets from him."

Junior showed interest for the first time since I had met the kid. Sandy looked skeptical.

"I thought you were ranching and raising horses," she said.

"I do. I'm not a detective or anything formal like that."

"He's being modest," Goodroe said. He told them the stories Warren Prew had heard from my father. Fourthhand like that, they sounded pretty exciting, but I wished the man had not done that. I wasn't paying any attention to Junior's reaction, but the girl was frowning.

"It all sounds very . . . unstable," she said. I got the impression that that had been the most polite way she could think of to put it. "What is Daddy paying you for this expertise, Mr. Heller?" she asked. A few minutes earlier it had been "Carl."

I shrugged.

Goodroe—why couldn't a grown man learn to keep petty details from his children?—explained. "So you see, if Carl can't help us, we will owe him nothing. I think it is awfully nice of him to invest his time in our problems with no guarantee of a return." He was smiling.

"Unstable," Sandy repeated.

"You could look at it that way."

"I do." She turned away and began concentrating on her Smith and Curry.

The rest of the evening I spent answering Junior's questions and marveling at the chill I could feel rising from Sandy's nicely formed, medium-tanned shoulders.

7

The Goodroe homestead turned out to be not exactly what I had expected. After seeing the plant and the expansion plans and the Fleetwood Brougham, I was expecting some grandiose sprawl of brick and glass in the Broadmoor or maybe Cheyenne Mountain area. Instead the Goodroes lived in a very nice but very normal four-bedroom house in the hilly northeast part of the city, not too awfully far from G&G Electronics. The view of the mountains would have been spectacular if it were not for the intervening rooftops and swing sets and television antennas. (I know better, but I always say "antennas.")

There wasn't any maid, either. And—I had been wondering—no Mrs. Goodroe. Goodroe's wife had died several years ago. The place was kept by Sandy, so she must have been the one I had spoken to on the telephone when I first got into town.

I took the opportunity to sleep in later than my usual early-morning chore call, something I will do any and every chance I get, but even so, the door to Junior's bedroom was still closed when I crept out with my shaving kit in my hand in search of a bathroom. (There is something awkward and vaguely intimidating about the use of a guest bathroom. It always makes me feel uncomfortable, although an equally strange john in a motel doesn't give that same sense of insecurity. Odd.)

Sandy was in the kitchen, but it turned out I had gotten up too late to see Goodroe. It wasn't quite eight o'clock yet but he had already left for the office.

"Daddy said to tell you he would meet you at the plant. He said you could ride in with Junior."

I nodded and accepted a cup of coffee from her. I had to

38

finally ask for an ashtray because none were in evidence anywhere around the place. "If you don't mind, that is," I added, hoping there would be no objection. I've been in plenty of homes where a persnickety hausfrau wasn't too shy to object to a guest's nasty smoke. I think the modern attitude is that us smokers are supposed to fall all over ourselves with admiration for their self-control and human rights and all that good stuff. Personally it just hacks me off. I'm hooked on the things and enjoy them too much to quit even if I thought I could, which is debatable.

The girl made no objections and went to the appropriate cupboard. "What do you want for breakfast?"

"I don't want to put you to any trouble," I told her.

"If I regarded it as a source of trouble I wouldn't have made the offer. Besides, you are my father's guest. Eggs and bacon?"

"That sounds fine." Hell, I wasn't going to quarrel with her. She made the words sound like an arsenic season-ing on the eggs would be a fine idea if that wouldn't be an affront to her pappy. I sat at the kitchen table and smoked and drank my coffee and became very well acquainted with the view of the mountains beyond their redwood deck. After an appropriate amount of pot rattling she put the food in front of me.

"Could I ask you something?" I asked before she could turn away.

She didn't answer, but she didn't leave either. She stood there waiting.

"Have I done something to offend you? I mean, yester-day evening you were all easygoing smiles and laughter. This morning you have your shell drawn up way past your ears. If I said anything . . ."

"You didn't," she said crisply.

"But I should keep my mouth shut and my questions to myself?"

Her face remained calm but her eyes said she was on the fringes of real anger. She pulled out a chair across the table and sat to give me a level gaze.

"There is a great deal you do not know about me, Mr. Heller, but I have had an absolute belly full of wanderers and dabblers, of men who do a little of this and a little of

that and can't bear the thought of settling down to reality."
The anger was bubbling closer to the surface now. Whatever it was that was bugging her was *really* bothersome.

"I am twenty-four years old, Mr. Heller, and I spent
three of those years, unwonderful years I might add, married to a man who was very much like you. A dabbler.
'Ne'er-do-well' is what they used to call it. Now I understand why they called it that. He used to pretend to be a
gallant visionary in search of greater truths than the mundane,
everyday world could provide. When I was nineteen that
was a wonderfully exciting concept. By the time I was
twenty I learned that that was all it was, a pretense, and all
it ever would be. A ne'er-do-well is a ne'er-do-well by any
other name. Much like a rose, Mr. Heller. So I've learned
my lesson, the hard way. I don't find people like you to be
at all exciting or mysterious or glamorous. Shiftless, yes,
but hardly glamorous.

"You are a guest in my father's house, and I will treat
you with the courtesy that is required. You are trying to
help my father, and I will answer truthfully any question
you put to me. But don't expect me to *like* you too. Your
eggs are getting cold."

What I should have told her was how much I appreci-
ated and understood her candor and her honesty. I should
have encouraged her to talk it all out and tell me everything about it. I should have given her some explanations
about justice and truth and—how does the rest of that
phrase go?—the American way of life.

Unfortunately it was about fifteen minutes later when I
finally got all my responses worked out, and by then she
had gone off to some other part of the house.

In the meantime I sat with a large glob of figurative egg
on my face and busied myself with stuffing some actual
egg into it.

She had been dead-on accurate about one thing, though.
The eggs were cold.

8

Junior was in no particular hurry to get to the plant, whatever it was he did there to justify the confusion about which Mr. Goodroe I had been asking for. It was past nine before he finished eating the breakfast he had prepared for himself—no short-order service for brothers, it seemed—and pronounced himself ready to go.

The kid's car was a turbocharged (it's all the rage these days, on two wheels or four) 300ZX, and he handled it like he was preparing himself for the Pikes Peak Hill Climb. I don't mean that he drove it badly, far from it, but he sure favored the "go" pedal over the other one.

I got the impression that he wanted to impress me. He sure kept looking my way and grinning a lot.

Actually he could have saved himself the trouble and saved his dad the gas and rubber bills. My favored form of transportation is on top of two very rapid wheels, and to anyone who bikes and has outgrown the moped stage, a car, any car, is closer to a slug than a bullet—if I can borrow that most explanatory phrase from the Kawasaki ads.

I will say this for his driving style, it would have made the commuting time no big deal. Except that it turned out we weren't headed for the plant yet.

"Isn't that the way to the office?" I asked when we breezed by the road I had taken the day before.

"Yeah." He grinned at me. "Are you a video freak?"

I didn't know what the hell he was talking about. "I don't even know what one of those critters is," I told him.

"Come on. You mean you don't play?"

"Somehow," I said, "I don't think you're using the same definition I would apply to that term, Junior."

41

"Man, you are in for a treat." He zipped the silver Datsun into the lot of a small shopping center and brought it chirping to a spring-rocking halt in front of a defunct convenience market that now wore a hand-painted sign saying "Game Room" on its facade. "Video games, Carl. That's the thing these days." He was still grinning. "That's what I'm doing at G&G, you know."

I shook my head. I hadn't known. Still didn't, for that matter.

"I'm working on a video-game program. We'll have to go through one of the majors to market it, of course. Atari or one of those. But when I get it worked out and copyrighted it'll be a whale of a big seller. Just wait and see. Video games are where it's at."

I think I winced a little. Video games I know from nothing, but phrases like "where it's at" have a tendency to bother me.

Come to think of it, that's a pretty poor attitude for a grown man to take. Put me with some friends behind the chutes at some rodeo, and I'll talk country as all hail. Queue me up with a bunch of dirt daubers at the scoring table of an enduro meet, and my language will smell of castor oil and two-stroke engines. Let me pull into a highway rest area beside a bunch of spike-helmeted Harley riders and I'll meet their lingo too. And never think a thing about it in any of those cases.

So I guess I don't have any right to feel offended however Junior might choose to sully the Queen's English. I do the same thing myself in other ways.

We went into the game room, and Junior began feeding five-dollar bills into a coin changer. He got twenty dollars' worth of quarters and handed a fistful of them to me.

"You'll understand what I'm doing better if you play some of these games," he said.

I looked around and discovered that the choices were bewildering.

The game room was filled with ranks of electronic machinery that winked and blinked and—I swear—even *talked* for crying out loud. There was one of the damn things that kept hollering "help me, help me" at the customers.

This was midmorning, now, but the place was nearly filled. Some of the clientele was made up of the teenagers I would have expected from the little I've read on the subject of the video-game phenomenon. What surprised me was that there were so many grown people, including a couple middle-aged men in business suits. It was an amazement indeed.

The games themselves were even more of an amazement.

I think I had been expecting something on the order of the pinball machines that I had had a brief but passionate affair with when I was a kid.

What these things were was *Star Wars* come to life, damn near.

Junior pointed me toward one called Astro Blaster, with an explanation that it was pretty simple and self-explanatory. You just shoot down the "enemy" when and where you see him. Easy to do, he said. You bet.

I plugged a quarter into the machine. Junior gave me a grin and went off to some more exciting game.

Shee-oot!

I think my quarter lasted a half-minute or maybe less. The critters were shooting back at me. I'd try to dodge one torpedo or laser or rocket or whatever they were supposed to be, and another would get me. My squadron of three spaceships was used up almost before I figured out how to fire my guns.

Another quarter gave me some practice, though, and then I figured I had it whipped. Why, there weren't but so many of the rascals, and I could whup 'em. A bunch of little orange extraterrestrials weren't going to get the best of Carl Heller, nossir.

I put another coin into the greedy machine and went to shooting.

Sure enough, I had it taped. I wiped those suckers out and only lost one of my own ships doing it. Figured I had this stuff *cold*.

Huh. As soon as the orange ones were splashed, here came another whole fleet of different ships, and *they* were shooting at me too.

I couldn't seem to get them so easily, and after a couple

more quarters I got curious about the game, wondered just
how far a fella had to go to beat the machine.

Just for the heck of it I beckoned to a pimply-faced
youngster wearing the colors of a fast-food chain I'd seen
down the block. He looked like a whiz at these things, so I
told him I'd stake him to a game if he'd show me how far
you had to go to be a clear winner. The kid gave me an
odd look.

"Are you serious, mister?"

I assured him that I was.

"Man, you *never* run out of play on these things. You
just keep going as long as you have ships left." He was
being honest with me, but he wasn't going to let a free
game escape, either. He stepped in front of the machine
and held out his hand for a quarter. "I've seen guys better
than me, but I can show you a few layers into it."

Heck, that game had mother ships and docking maneu-
vers and extra fuel if you shot down flaming comets in the
midst of meteor showers and . . . Weird stuff. I had never
lasted long enough to learn that you could run out of fuel
as well as out of ships, but this kid could handle it all. He
docked with the "mother" ship and refueled several times
before some bird-looking things finally got him. He looked
at me and smiled. "See?"

I shook my head.

Amazement indeed.

The whole thing seemed fairly pointless to my way of
thinking, but obviously these people—and they weren't
just kids, either—were getting something out of it. Maybe
what I lacked for comprehension was a life-style that has
no fear or insecurity in it. Maybe this was an outlet for
them, a sort of surrogate destructiveness that let them
release their tensions harmlessly on a computerized battle
to the death.

I found myself grinning at one Carl Heller, do-it-yourself
psychologist. Half an hour in a game room, and I had the
whole thing down pat, as to motive if not to method.

I thanked my helpful guide, gave him some more quarters to play with, and went wandering down the aisles of
fancy machines.

Some were set up like mazes, some—like the one I'd

been playing—in outer space, several like racetracks, tank combat, WWI aerial combat, submarines sinking ships. One even had a *Jaws* theme with sharks attacking scuba divers, who shrieked whenever they were bitten. That one, I was amazed to discover, had the "good" guy as the *shark*, for crying out loud. They gave your shark "thrust" and "munch" controls, and the object of the game was to attack and eat the humans before they could spear you. Ghoulish, I tell you, right down to the agonized screams. I wondered how Junior Goodroe was going to compete with the mastermind who had come up with that one.

Still, there was no question but that somebody was raking in fortunes from these machines. Until the fad passed, owning the copyright to a video game would have to be the next best thing to government permission to print your own money.

Junior played at least an hour and a half, hopping from machine to machine instead of parking himself in front of a favorite the way most of the customers seemed to do. But then, he was here on a purely research project on behalf of good old Glen's corporate interests. I had to keep reminding myself of that. Not that I succeeded in fully convincing myself, but I came close a time or two. Eventually he ran out of quarters.

"What do you think?" he asked as we headed back toward the silver four-wheeler.

"About the games? They're . . . different. I don't really know what I expected. Certainly the age range of the customers surprised me. Is it like that all over?"

"Sure. Everybody plays video games now." He was grinning. A happy young fellow, Junior Goodroe. "Would you like to hear about my game?"

I nodded. I didn't think I would have much choice anyway, so I might just as well concede without a fuss.

"It's going to be really keen. I mean *really*." He cranked the engine over and cut in the afterburners. "Progressive difficulty, of course. Basically it's an obstacle course. You launch these astronauts out of a mother ship, see. It's on the surface of the moon. I'm researching the Apollo landing sites to get that right. Anyway, you start your astronauts from this lunar lander thing, but the Martians or somebody have set up this really neat minefield and fields of laser fire and . . .''

He kept going, but I pretty much quit listening. I mean, it is one thing to play one of those games. The concept behind them really was more than I wanted to know.

But then, I've been stupid before and I likely will be again.

9

The employees at G&G were an awfully easygoing crowd. I had to take Glen's and Junior's word that they were good at their jobs, since I didn't know enough about what any of them were doing to begin to understand it. To me—and I suppose this is an admission of sorts—they just seemed awfully damned *young*. A bunch of fresh-faced kids busy at this and that mysterious work.

But they were sure relaxed and comfortable with it. They seemed to always have time for a cup of tea, more popular with this set than coffee for some reason, or to play Junior a video game on one of their in-house computers.

I chatted a bit with them, just friendly stuff, trying to show an interest in their work, and while all of them were open about it, none of them displayed any particular interest in or knowledge about the Rainbow Drive.

That, of course, was being handled by Glen Goodroe with the help of a single assistant, who was just as bright as the others but a whole lot prettier. She was about Sandy's age, and from the way Junior reacted to her—cool if not quite openly hostile—I wondered if she and Goodroe might have something more than a professional involvement. Still, that was only guessing. No one actually said or did anything to indicate it.

During the days, I followed Junior around the plant, playing his games with him and trying to be polite about his ten thousand questions. The boy had an awful lot of interest in the things I might have done for others in the past, and I had to keep on my toes to keep from telling him anything, without being offensive.

That is not a subject I like to talk much about anyway, and Junior was too young and too unsettled to trust with that kind of conversation even if I didn't have a close-mouthed habit.

I was put off a little too because friendly conversation and interest from Junior Goodroe seemed faintly out of place. The employees at G&G were a genuinely relaxed and friendly group, but with Junior there was a flavor of politeness in the way they treated him, and his responses to them carried a rather more distinct flavor of superiority. Something to do with being G. Goodroe Jr., I gathered. I was getting the impression that he was more than a bit spoiled. I wouldn't go so far as to say that the kid was a snot, but I did begin to get tired of the toothy grin that he was always showing me and those constant questions.

But then, maybe he just needed someone to buddy up with and couldn't bring himself to make friends with a lowly peon on an employee level.

At night I would have welcomed some conversation.

Junior disappeared nightly immediately following supper, and Goodroe had what I gathered was a long-standing habit of bringing work home from the office.

Which left me with Sandy, short for Alexandra.

Damn but that was one fine-looking female. And just as distant as she was attractive.

Postdinner conversation with her was mostly mono-syllabic, me trying to be bright and friendly on the one hand and she fending me off on the other. Even a mutual interest in horseflesh wasn't enough to arouse any sparks of interest and, hell, it just isn't much fun to regale the throngs with tales of ancient rodeo derring-do when nobody's listening.

After a couple nights I gave up on it and began investigating the family-room bookshelves to pass the time.

I didn't find it particularly flattering that Sandy seemed to so thoroughly approve of that decision.

On Friday I decided there was little or no point in wasting Glen Goodroe's time and mine. I didn't think my kind of prying could do him much good when a bunch of pros had failed.

"I'm sorry, Glen, but I'm not doing a thing here except wasting your time and imposing on your hospitality."

He looked up from the pile of accordion-folded printout material he had been looking at. "Are you sure, Carl?"

I shrugged. The only thing I was sure of was that I wasn't accomplishing a damn thing here. I tried to soften it with a smile. "At least I don't think you're paranoid. I think my dad was lucky to have nice people for friends."

That brought a polite return smile. "Are you in any hurry to get home?" he asked.

I shook my head.

"Then I'd like to have dinner with you this evening before you leave. Would that be all right?"

"I'd enjoy it."

He looked at his watch and frowned. "Could I meet you there?" He named the restaurant. "About six-thirty?"

"Sure. That would give me time to stop by the house and pick up my things. I can head on up the pass after dinner."

"Good enough. Tell Sandy for me that I won't be home for dinner tonight. And would you ask Cathy to make a reservation for us? It is Friday night, after all."

I nodded. For some reason everybody in the Springs seems to eat out on Friday nights. Up in the mountains practically no one eats out on Fridays, probably because we get in the habit of wanting to avoid the tourists and city dwellers. Up above, Tuesdays and Thursdays are the big nights for dining out with Ma and the kids.

I passed the word at the receptionist's desk and waved so long to Junior. As usual he was noodling with a computer keyboard with one eye on the CRT screen and the other on Cathy's well-turned ankles, which was all you could see of her under the privacy screen of her desk.

Alexandra, predictably, was underwhelmed at the thought of losing my companionship. She didn't say anything about where or why I might be going, and neither did I. I just packed my gear, got directions from her about how to reach the right place, and got into the Jeep. I was feeling . . . let down. Plain and simple. Like I wasn't a whole hell of a lot of good myself or to anybody else.

The place Goodroe had named was well out Garden of the Gods Road, past the burgeoning Electronics Row where so many space-age companies have come in in the past few years to manufacture calculators and Space Shuttle components and I have no idea what all else. It seems to be quite a field, but at least it is clean and keeps our unemployment rates low.

Anyway, I was early for the dinner with Goodroe so I stopped into a lounge on the way and had a Coors Light to help pass the time. It got rid of the time but not the mood as I sat there and nursed my way through several of the things. When the trusty Timex said it was time, I paid and got out of there before I could get maudlin.

The restaurant was set well back off the road, its exterior only dimly lighted in the dusk. It was one of those understated and probably quite excellent places that sees no reason to shout its existence. That frequently indicates the kind of restaurant whose customers will search it out, and I was almost looking forward to the meal.

The parking area was already nearly full, which was another good sign, and I had to leave the Jeep around back, where there were still a few slots left. I decided it was a good thing Goodroe had made reservations.

There is no point in trying to lock a soft-top Jeep, so I threw a scrungy, cast-off army blanket over my bag and tried not to think about it being unprotected. The evening was chilly and there was a wind picking up, which tends to drive the cold to the bone, so I tugged my Stetson lower and took a wrap around my belly with the sport coat and headed at a brisk but dignified walk toward the door. (What kind of stubbornness is it in a man that will force him to choose discomfort over the indignity of a run in bad weather? Whatever it is, I'm afflicted; I will *not* allow a little rain or snow or cold to make me change my pace.)

A couple other customers were getting out of their car in front of me, and I noticed before I ducked my head against the wind that maybe I had overestimated this place. Neither of them was dressed the way I would have expected. They were wearing workclothes. Of course jeans are more or less accepted just about anyplace these days, but still . . . I hustled on past.

Whatever it was the sonuvabitch hit me with, the brim of my Stetson did little to soften the blow.

I felt the impact *inside* my head, not on the surface, so i was one hard and serious swing. It's the really bad ones that come inside and jolt you where you live. The penny-ante punches stay out there on the skin where they land.

All of a sudden I was one happy, uninterested fella, sort of watching it all happen from a distant, detached point of view.

My legs were wobbly and I was reeling. I knew it but I didn't particularly care. From the descriptions I've had, I would say the feeling must be something like the kids' experience when they float away on a cloud of chemicals. But I don't recommend this method of getting there.

Oddly enough, I was more aware of sounds than of physical sensations.

I could hear a loud, grunting exhalation of breath as one of them hooked a real crusher into my kidneys. I was aware of being hit, sort of, but I was much more interested in the quality and the volume of the sound.

I could hear the dull thumps of impact as they laid into me with fists or maybe clubs of some kind. The word "cosh" came into mind and I found that to be teddibly English and teddibly amusing. I was able to keep myself from giggling. Dignity, you know. I must have *really* taken a hit to the head to be wanting to giggle while two guys were busily beating the shit out of me.

The thumping didn't last too long, and then I seemed to be floating for a while. I couldn't figure that out at first, but something was tugging at the heels of my boots. Eventually I decided I was being dragged and wasn't floating after all.

Ha ha. They fooled you, Carl. Good joke on you, old boy.

There was a little breathless conversation—they really weren't in very good shape if they had trouble dragging a body for that little bit of time—that had something to do with wondering if I was alive or dying. They didn't seem to particularly care either way, and neither did I at the moment. I was feeling sleepy and wanted them to put me down.

It was so nice of them. They did put me down. In front of my CJ. I recognized the winch and the grille. I think I smiled at them, or tried to.

Very kind of them.

I drifted into a warm, comfortable sleep.

10

"Damn you."

I gave him my very best attempt at a smile, but I don't think it was very good. "Now what?"

"That tune you were humming. It just keeps going through my head, and I can't remember what it is. It's driving me crazy."

This time I think the smile was somewhat better. Glen Goodroe had heard and found me because, out though I was, I seem to have been lying there half under the front bumper of my Jeep humming a tune. Incredible. I damn sure didn't feel like humming *now*.

"Give me a few bars," I said. He did. I smiled at him again. " 'Faster Horses.' Tom T. Hall. It's one of my favorite philosophical lyrics of all time." Goodroe looked like he did not remember it. "It says that all of life is a search for faster horses and younger women and older whiskey and more money. Very profound."

"You believe that?"

"There are times. But I think you should add vengeance, too. That's one of the basic pleasures of life also." I was stretched out in the bed in Goodroe's guest room on a bright Saturday morning. I was trying very hard to avoid thinking about what would have happened last night if Goodroe had not heard me humming my happy tune. The temperature hadn't been all that low, but then, hypothermia doesn't require low temps. A breeze and sustained cool temperatures will kill you just as dead as a more dramatic freeze-dry method. It would be something of an understatement to say that I was grateful to the guy.

As it happened, though, the damage was neither permanent nor extreme. I was woozy as hell and was informed that my lower back was a study in shades of purple, but nothing had happened that wouldn't go away, given a little time.

"I hope this had nothing to do with your being here on my behalf," Goodroe said. He was obviously thinking about the beating.

"I'm sure it didn't," I lied.

Actually I couldn't think of any other reason. I mean, the city streets are rough these days. But *that* rough? I didn't think so. "I would like to stay here and rest up for a little while," I added. "Would you mind if I went to sleep now?"

Goodroe excused himself and left for whatever pursuits he undertook on a Saturday at home.

I lay there not at all sleepy and did some thinking. I had seen the men who jumped me, of course, but I wasn't entirely sure that I could remember them if I saw them again.

To begin with, they had been of absolutely no interest to me when they got out of that car, and I'd had my head down against the wind. The light had been poor and the parking area nearly free of artificial light. And after they hit me I sure hadn't been thinking about anything like identifying them. Hadn't cared about it at all right then.

But I sure did now. I surely would like to have a word or two with those boys.

Who they were, though, wasn't really bothering me all that much for the time being.

I was also wondering why they jumped me and how they knew where to do it.

Why? I shook my head, then regretted that. The movement caused my dull aches to flare into active pains from the shoulders down to my waist. Most uncomfortable, this healing.

Why. If I knew anything anybody should be worried about, I sure as hell didn't know it. As far as I was concerned I'd gained not an inch on whoever was doing a job on Glen Goodroe and G&G Electronics.

On the other hand, it seemed more and more likely to me now that Goodroe was no paranoid. He believed someone was snitching his trade secrets, and now I was willing to believe him. Before, that had been of only incidental interest, a subject that might or might not be true and that I didn't really care about one way or the other. He had asked me to look and so I was looking. Now I was believing him. And was developing a personal interest in the matter.

I thought back over everything I'd learned about Goodroe and about his business. When you boiled it down I had learned very little. Certainly nothing that I could think of as significant. I shelved that question for the time being.

How? That was the next one.

There I had more choices. The receptionist, Cathy, was the one who had made the reservation. She could have mentioned it to anyone else in the office. If not in casual chatter, then in an innocent answer to anybody's question. It was a free-and-easy crowd at the plant, and any one of them could find a hundred excuses to ask where the boss was dining with his guest that night. No one else would think twice about answering.

So the list of possibles in the "who" category was as long as the payroll.

That was a big help, I decided. Clever me, I congratulated myself. You've really narrowed the field, Carl.

I sighed. Maybe sleep wasn't such a bad idea after all.

Sunday I felt up to a long hike. All the way from the bedroom to the living room. It was a major accomplishment.

Goodroe was lost inside a pile of papers with an expensive-looking calculator at his elbow, and Junior was gone somewhere for the day. Which left me with a choice of Sandy or the television set. I automatically opted for the TV, marveling as always at the fact that down here in the flat country you could actually get a sharp, clear picture on a television screen.

The Broncos played at eleven A.M., an away game, and managed to lose a squeaker to a last-minute field goal. I wondered if I should call the day a bad deal and go back to bed.

Dallas was playing the second game, though, and I will happily root for anybody trying to whip the Cowboys. I don't think it is their arrogance that makes my bile rise.

Hell, they're entitled to that. I think it is their name. Cowboys. The only one who was entitled to that was Walt Garrison, and he's long since retired to more lucrative pastures.

Anyway, I got to whooping and hollering as soon as the Redskins kicked off. Couldn't help myself.

A couple minutes later the Cowpersons fumbled, and I heard Sandy groan and cuss some under her breath.

"Don't tell me you're a fan."

"Of course. Any sensible person is."

I snorted. "Which proves a very old point. Anyone who would admit to being a Dallas Cowboys fan doesn't have the judgment needed to cast a ballot." I grinned. "My granddad always said we had no business giving women the vote. Maybe he was right."

All right, maybe I was baiting her a bit, but why not. Being pleasant and helpful sure hadn't gotten me anywhere.

She rose to the bait like a trout in the nymph hatch, and we were off on a fifteen-minute discourse that fell just short of being an argument.

For a homebody who was substituting as her father's hausfrau she was able to generate some sharp, effective arguments. I hadn't given much thought to the girl's mind—my interests, frankly, being concentrated on her body instead—but she had a better quality of gray matter between her ears than I would have expected.

It made me wonder if I had been underestimating Miss Alexandra Goodroe. *Mrs.* Alexandra Whatever, actually. It occurred to me that I didn't know what her married name had been. Nowadays she was going under her maiden name again, I gathered.

There was a lot I didn't know about the girl anyway.

And then it occurred to me that there was something else I did know about her.

Alexandra was the person who'd given me directions how to get to the restaurant the other night.

So my list of possibles was at least one name longer.

And while she had been nice and pleasant and talkative that first evening at Bob Young's Cabaret, once she found out who I was and why I was down here, she had sure changed her tune.

Ever since that moment she had been unfriendly if not actively antagonistic.

It made me wonder.

I got so interested in that train of thought that I forgot to bring the ceiling down with my cheering when the 'Skins put a hurtin' on the Cowboys. That is an oversight I don't often make.

11

By Tuesday I was feeling damn near human, and Sandy, who had been acting damn near pleasant the last couple days, offered to get me out of the house for a change of scenery. I will admit that I was more than weary of game shows and daytime soap operas.

"I have to go out there anyway," she said, "so it isn't like I'd be making a special trip just on your behalf." She was referring to the pasture/expansion site north of town where her horses had plenty of grass to keep their bellies full but where it was wise to keep an eye on the windmill to make sure they didn't run out of water. "Besides, the exercise will be good for you."

She was right about that. I was still hobbling about like a ninety-seven-year-old arthritic, and I really needed to force some movement of the abused and loudly protesting muscles. "If you're sure it wouldn't be a bother."

"Of course not." She even smiled.

Brother's vehicle was the hard-driven, turbocharged sportsy-box, but hers turned out to be a gleamingly new and highly polished but nevertheless utilitarian Toyota 4 × 4 pick-'em-up truck. It was a cute little rascal, and she handled it competently. To tell the truth, I felt more comfortable riding with her than I had with her brother.

"Daddy tells me you're thinking about staying on now," she mentioned casually as we followed the curves of U.S. 83. "I thought you were on your way home."

"Oh, I might stay around some," I said just as casually. My suspicions, though, were in high gear. Here was a girl who hadn't been willing to give me the right time of day before. Now all of a sudden she was showing a concerned interest that seemed out of place after what had gone before.

57

And I couldn't help remembering that it was after this girl told he how to get to that parking lot that a couple fellows just happened to be on hand with a desire to rearrange my insides. Coincidences are something I don't put a lot of stock in.

"Do you think you might be onto something that would help us?" she asked. She gave every appearance of having her attention on the road before us, but I didn't put a whole hell of a lot of stock in that either.

I shrugged. "I really don't know." The truth, of course, was that I hadn't a thing more now than I had the week before when I was willing to pack it in and go home. But if someone else—like Miss Alexandra there—*thought* I did, well, why should I turn my back on an opportunity like that? "I'll poke around some more and find out."

"Do you want to talk about it?" She glanced away from the road long enough to give me a brief, questioning look. An invitation to share my burdens if I so desired.

A suspicious man, I thought, might take that to be a sign of an unnatural interest, considering the way she had been regarding me before.

And there are those who say that I am a suspicious kind of person. Not trusting worth a damn.

Spill your guts out to the sympathetic, pretty lady, Carl, go right ahead. You bet.

I shook my head. "Not yet."

She didn't press it, and a few silent minutes later we reached Goodroe's property. Sandy got the gate herself rather than ask me to crawl groaning and whimpering out of the truck and back in again, and we drove cross-country up to the windmill and stock tank on the back side of the tract.

"Daddy must be getting closer to starting construction," she said as we passed some small piles of freshly disturbed earth where somebody had been doing some core drillings or some such preconstruction activity.

"You don't know?" I asked.

She smiled. "He knows I have no interest in the business. He doesn't bore me with talking about it all the time at home."

She didn't sound particularly resentful when she said

that, but I couldn't help wondering if she was feeling left out of her father's life. Left out and resentful enough, maybe, to make her want him to fail at it? It was an interesting question.

It was a shot in the dark, of course, but *every* kid gets mad at *every* parent at one time or another. Real mad. Most don't go to retaliatory extremes the way somebody was doing with Glen Goodroe. But the desire exists in all of us at one time or another. We'll run away from home and never be seen again or, boy, we'll *really* show 'em; we'll get real sick an' just *die*, by damn. Then where would they be? We outgrow all that, of course, but I wondered what would happen if the experience was delayed until adult methods were available for the satisfaction of juvenile desires. It seemed a definite possibility, if not necessarily the most likely one. That remained to be seen.

I sighed a little and must admit that I was getting a bit amused with myself. Carl Heller, do-it-yourself shrink. Maybe I should make like Lucy and put up a roadside stand: "The Doctor Is *In*. 5¢ per Visit." You bet.

The Toyota rocked and quivered to a halt beside the stock tank, and Sandy hopped lightly out to make sure everything was as it should be. I was somewhat slower in my gingerly descent. I was getting a bit tired of aches and pains.

"Is it okay?" I asked. I really didn't want to walk around and see for myself.

"Just fine," she answered brightly.

The horses came over and inspected her pockets in search of handouts, and she didn't disappoint them. She fed them something from her hand and rubbed their polls.

"Are you in a hurry?" she asked.

"Not hardly."

She got a double-bitted English bridle from the back of the truck and strapped a postage-stamp saddle onto the bay horse. She had herself a bit of a canter while I hobbled around and tried to pretend that I was feeling better. I darn sure declined when she offered to let me ride one of her pets.

12

Wednesday I drove myself to the G&G plant, and I had to admit that the activity did seem to be making me feel somewhat better. Man, I always envy those ol' boys on the TV who can have the crap beat out of them and take only a commercial break to be feeling themselves again. It must be a real pleasure. Or maybe a real poor script.

Glen and his assistant were closeted in the research room doing something that no one was supposed to know about, which Junior explained to me with a trace of bitterness in his tone of voice. I got the impression that it wasn't the work but maybe the assistant that was bugging him. That was natural enough, I guess. He was still young enough and certainly immature enough to find revolting any hint that his very own daddy might have some physical yens below the beltline.

Glen Goodroe was a helluva fine man, but I was having some doubts about his kids.

Anyway, I played Junior's partially worked-out video game for a while, and I had to agree with him that he had a just-fine view of papa's secretary from where he liked to sit. She was prime. I couldn't say as much about the game he was trying to put together, but then, I am no expert on that subject. For all I knew, it might be the greatest thing since Pac-Man.

After a little of that, which seemed like a lot and taxed pretty heavily my ability to be complimentary without actual lying, I excused myself with the explanation that I had some things to check out.

Which was true enough. I wasn't about to get specific with Junior. It was his sister I was wanting to check out, and not the same way I might have wanted to a week or so earlier.

My Jeep is too conspicuous for what I had in mind so I looked up the friendly local We Try Harder folks. Half an hour later I had possession of a citified form of camouflage, a silver-gray Honda Accord. It made me long for the days when cars resembled gunboats but had some man-sized room inside them. Still, there are so many Japanese cheeseboxes on the road these days that no one pays any attention to them even if he is one of those rare types who can tell one from another.

I found a sunny spot a block and half from the Goodroe home where I could keep an eye on the place and, armed with a paper cup of coffee and a sack of 7-11 sandwiches, began a vigil.

I can state on good authority that on Wednesday, Alexandra Goodroe tended her knitting—or whatever it was she was doing in the otherwise empty household—and stayed home.

Early Thursday afternoon, this time with a copper-colored Fiat for my in-town camo, I watched the young lady wheel out of the driveway and head for—it was thrilling—a shopping center. Big deal. I parked a suitable distance away and watched while she went into King Soopers for a cart of groceries. It was hard to keep from yawning.

She was back forty-five minutes later and set her groceries into the back of the truck. I was still yawning.

She made a face and made a bit of a production of snapping her fingers. Forgot something, she was telling the world. She left her grocery cart sitting where it was— people who leave carts in the middle of otherwise empty parking slots always vex me—and hurried back toward the grocery store.

There was a public telephone outside, and she made use of it.

What's this? I wondered. The lady has a perfectly good telephone minutes away and probably has frozen foods in those bags too. Clever me. I wondered if there was a plot thickening.

The girl stood waiting beside the telephone for some time, twenty minutes at least I would say, looking nervously this way and that the entire wait. I slouched low in the Fiat's seat and came up with at least fifty possible reasons for what she was doing there, both plausible and otherwise.

After a while a white van pulled to a stop nearby, and Sandy ran around to the driver's window. She talked for only a moment to the guy before he reached out and handed her something, I couldn't see what.

There was that very brief exchange and then the van pulled away. Sandy headed briskly back toward her Toyota and haul of groceries, and the van headed quickly for an exit from the lot.

Curious, I thought.

The van wheeled down the parking aisle next to the one where I was parked, coming much closer to me on its way out. There is nothing unusual about a bored husband waiting in a car outside a grocery store, so I sat where I was and watched the guy come nearer. I hadn't been able to get a good look at the driver yet, and I wanted to.

The van swept past and . . . *Jesus!* I wasn't sure. I wasn't entirely positive.

But I would almost swear that the face behind that open side window was one of the guys I had seen once before. In another parking lot. Just before those same two guys jumped me from behind and did their very best to beat the shit out of an annoyance named Carl Heller.

I felt a pang of what must have been regret of sorts. A combination of things all mixed together that I didn't have time to sort out at the moment. Things like a liking for Glen Goodroe and a sadness for Sandy Goodroe and fleeting thoughts about love and loyalty and familial affections and . . . I don't know what all else.

Hell, I should have been happy. When a pet hunch pays off, it should be cause for rejoicing. I couldn't be all that pleased about it, actually. I would much rather have been totally wrong about Miss Alexandra Goodroe, if only for Glen's sake. He deserved better.

But I didn't have time to get into a session of fret-and-fuss with myself.

I cranked the little Fiat and set out in un-hot pursuit of a gentleman driving a white delivery van. I wanted to know a great deal more about this fella.

13

The man, whoever he was, seemed to be working rather than lurking. He drove out to Electronics Row, not far from where those bastards had jumped me, and stopped at three different plants. Each time he went around to their loading docks and stopped only long enough to pick up some packages to load into the back of the van.

Delivery service of some sort, I thought. But it was reasonably certain that it was no business package he had delivered to Alexandra Goodroe. Whatever that had been, it was no larger than a note. Or currency. Come to think of it, I'd seen the meeting of hands and I had assumed that he was passing something to her. It could as easily have been the other way around. She might well have been giving him something. Or paying him something.

I followed him back across town to the airport on the southeast fringe of the city, and he parked this time at the Emery shipping dock.

There was no place to park where I could watch without being pretty obvious about it—and I had been behind him for quite a while now—so I buzzed on past without looking his way and found a place for the Fiat in the short-term lot.

The guy was busy unloading boxes and paper-wrapped parcels from the back of the van, stacking them onto a hand truck and hauling them inside. It was routine stuff to him, judging from the way he acted, but it gave me a chance to get a good look at him outside the confinement of the van.

He wasn't particularly big, no taller than I am, but he was in the kind of trim, fit physical condition that only the very wealthy or the very athletic maintain. Regular gym workouts would have been my guess. He had a very quick,

fluid way of moving that made me think of soccer or
legitimate wrestling rather than the football kind of physical ability.

He was wearing olive-colored workclothes, the kind you
can buy at K-Mart, with a patch over the right-breast shirt
pocket. I found myself wishing I was close enough to read
it.

His hair was dark and cut very short, and he was either
deeply tanned or fairly dark-complected, I couldn't decide
which. A heavy beard shadow by late afternoon, though,
made me suspect it would be the latter. I rubbed my own
facial fur and wondered if it would be a good idea for me
to start shaving again. Certainly I would be harder to spot
in a tail tomorrow if I shaved in the morning. Up home,
probably three-quarters of the men you see will be wearing
beards, but down here on the flat they aren't so common.

I was so busy thinking about that that I hardly noticed
him close and lock the back doors of the van, then fire it
up and drive quickly away.

I stood where I was and watched him go.

When the van was well out of sight I assumed my most
pleasant expression and jogged into the freight office,
puffing aloud more than I needed to.

"Say, dammit, I just missed him, but was that Pete
Carey that just pulled out of here? 'Bout so high? Dark?
Drives a white van?"

The clerk behind the counter looked up from his mani-
fest lists and looked puzzled for a moment. Then he
brightened. "Just now left here?"

I nodded.

The clerk shook his head. "Wrong man, mister, I'm
sorry."

This guy wasn't cooperating at all. What he was supposed to do was to blurt out the recently departed
gentleman's name, rank, and serial number, not just tell
me I had the wrong fellow in mind.

Besides, I'd already forgotten whatever last name I had
just given to my mythical friend.

"That sure looked like old Pete," I insisted. "Are you
positive it wasn't him?"

"Positive."

I stroked my beard. What the hell to do now? Damn all uncooperative dupes.

"The last I saw him, old Pete was having himself some hassle from his ex-wife. Do you think he could have changed his name 'cause of that?"

Aw, I admit it was pretty weak. It's just that that was the only thing I could think of at the moment. And who's to complain; it worked.

The shipping clerk looked up again with ill-concealed annoyance and got rid of me once and for all. "Look, mister, I don't know about this Pete friend of yours, but I can guarantee you that wasn't him. I've known Henry Blair for quite a while now, and I've heard him say he's never been married. Never. No ex-wife. No alimony. Nothing like that. Now, leave me be, will you?"

"Sure, sure thing. That, uh . . . what company is this Harry fella working for?"

"It's Henry," he corrected me with some sting in his voice. "Henry Blair. And he drives for Diplomat Courier Service. Now, will you let me get through this stuff? Please?"

"Sure, pal. Whatever you say. Sorry to have bothered you." I gave him a hokey grin. "You know how it is with old pals, though. Why, I could tell you stories about ol' Pete . . ."

The poor clerk looked like he was ready to cry.

"Hey, you don't want to hear all that. Sure. You have yourself a good day now, mister. I sure do thank you. Sure do."

I was still talking and smiling and bobbing my head when I got out the door.

No doubt the clerk was thinking I was an absolute idjit. Which was exactly what I wanted. A serious inquiry from a solid citizen he might be curious enough about to mention to good friend Harry Blair come tomorrow's deliveries.

But a bunch of lame chatter from such a garrulous idiot as I was, well, that he would gladly forget before dinnertime.

I whistled and hummed my way back to the too-small

Fiat and went off to reclaim my Jeep for the night. It wouldn't do to have anyone at the Goodroe household, in particular a pretty little female with medium-brown hair, notice the absence of that distinctive vehicle.

14

"Mr. Heller?" She sounded uncertain about that. I grinned at Glen Goodroe's girl Friday and rubbed my freshly shaved chin. It felt a little strange after I had gone and gotten used to the whiskers, but obviously it made a fair amount of difference in my appearance. I had also discarded my customary Stetson and was going bareheaded today. Believe me, that was a much bigger change than just lopping off some fur, at least as far as I was concerned. I felt plumb naked outdoors without a hat after so many years of wearing one. Felt cold and somehow vulnerable.

"It's me all right, Cathy."

"I almost didn't recognize you."

I grinned at her again. "Mind if I poke through the files some?"

"Of course not. Mr. Goodroe Senior said anything you want is what we want you to have."

For some reason I was reminded of a line from an old Henry Fonda/Glenn Ford movie. *Anything that suits you just tickles me plumb to death. The Rounders*, I think that one was. Terrific cowboy movie.

Anyhow, I prowled in the records some and found what I wanted easily enough. Diplomat Courier Service was employed by G&G on a contract basis. Daily pickup of outgoing parcels and delivery for shipment by common carrier. The contract specified up to twenty parcels daily at the flat rate, plus additional charges for any additional parcels or additonal pickups. The contract was nearly as old as G&G Electronics.

According to Cathy the same outfit serviced a number of local plants, but she had no idea which ones. Computer firms? Probably. Much of the city's light industry these days was computer or space-age stuff. I thanked her and wandered out.

I don't have anything like official contacts in Colorado Springs, but I do know a few people here and there. One of them happened to be a cop who is also an endurance rider and—I shudder when I think of it—ice racer. The guy is crazy as hell on two wheels, but he frequently finishes in front of me, so who am I to judge. I called the dispatch office, found out what area he was working in and left a message for him to meet me at the doughnut shop on South Circle. He pulled in not more than ten minutes after I got there.

"It's good to see you, Carl. Are you ready for the season to begin?"

"Begin hell, it just ended."

He laughed. He was actually looking forward to the lakes freezing hard enough to race on. That is a game I do not care to play. I keep having visions of steel-spiked tires tracking along my spine.

"Suit yourself."

"I'll come watch maybe, but you won't get me on one of those things."

He took a look at his watch. "If it isn't a racing schedule you need . . ."

I took the hint and told him what I wanted.

"No sweat." He stepped back outside to his patrol car and spoke into the radio. A couple minutes later he was back. "No record on a Henry Blair, Carl. Not even a traffic citation. Does that help?"

I shrugged. "It was worth a try."

"You're still, uh, monkeying where you have no business being?"

"I wouldn't do a thing like that, Tom."

"Yeah, I'll bet."

"Join me for a cup?"

He shook his head. "No time. I'll take a rain check."

"I owe you something. Collect it anytime."

He nodded and went back to work.

Whatever would a man do without friends? I wondered for perhaps the thousandth time.

*   *   *

Blair was easy enough to pick up again when I wanted him. I just waited at the airport until he made his daily stop at the Emery dock and tagged along from there, this time in a white Chevy Citation.

He returned the van to a very unimpressive set of Diplomat Courier offices and got into a definitely sharp-looking Chrysler convertible. Kinda snazzy for a delivery man, I thought.

His taste in transportation might be rather grand, but his eating habits seemed plebeian. He went to the Golden Arches and spent little time getting around whatever it was he ordered in there while I watched, hungry, from outside. From there he headed for South Nevada and the strip of joints and honky-tonks that cater to the GI trade from Fort Carson south of town. Gaudy lights, loud music, and an easy flow of cash is the order of the day down there.

The joint Henry favored was called the Cat's Meow and from the outside was hardly distinguishable from any of the others. Plenty of garish neon flashing the message that there were twenty—count 'em, twenty—beautiful ladies inside who would dance in a nude revue for your very own pleasure. It sounded just thrillin'.

I gave Henry about ten minutes to get settled and then carefully locked the doors of the little Citation before I followed him inside. Places like that do not generate much confidence in one's fellowman.

The inside of the place was as dark as I had hoped. Blacklight around the walls made the "artwork" practically bat you over the head. Line drawings of naked women done in fluorescent paints on black velvet. Gold and orange and yellow and some in red. None, thank goodness, in green. That would have been a bit much to take.

Most of the interior lighting came from a row of lights recessed above the bar and from a couple twirling starlight globes with small spots played on them. The rest came from the very intense spots that were centered over a raised runway and stage area that extend from the end of the bar far into the floor space.

What really got me, though, much more than the need to adjust my vision, was the damn music.

Walking inside that door was like pushing into a pile of pillows. The music was so loud it had a physical presence to it. I felt like I should be wading through it and not just walking.

The heavy *thump-ta-thump-ta-thump-thump-thump* of the beat drove through clothing and flesh and settled somewhere in the bones. I could feel it vibrating deep inside me. This might be some guys' idea of great vibes, but it bothered me. If I hadn't had a good reason for staying, I would have turned and gotten the hell out of there.

I was still standing there blinking my eyes against the darkness, popping my jaw in a futile attempt to clear my ears, and wondering if there were trolls and beasties lurking in the corners, when I felt a ghostly presence at my side.

I blinked a couple more times and the ghost became a half-seen figure with long blond hair and sultan's harem outfit of flowing see-through material. Probably in deference to the name of the place she had some long cat's whiskers painted on her cheeks. I believe this was supposed to be cute. Or something.

She leaned close and took my hand. Her touch was very soft and managed to convey a sense of intimacy. A whiff of perfume in a surprisingly delicate scent floated around her. She leaned even closer, and I could see her mouth move. Being as bright as your average bear, I concluded that she must be speaking to me.

I shook my head. Whatever she was trying to say didn't have a chance against all that *thump, thump, thump*.

She came up on her tiptoes and drew my head down until I could feel her breath in my ear. I can't say that I minded that part of it.

"Would you like a table or do you want to sit at the stage?"

Darn, and I thought she was hot for my body. Well, I've been dealt worse blows.

I blinked some more and found that my eyes were finally adjusting. There were some tables in the room that more or less offered privacy for one's imbibing and ogling, but most of the customers in the place were ranked on small chairs set the very edge of the runway. A dropped lip or shelf along the sides of the runway and stage gave them a place to set their glasses while they got an up-close look at the dancers.

My man Henry was among them.

I placed my lips near the blond's ear. Her closeness and that perfume were having an amazing amount of impact, I discovered. "A table, I think. How 'bout over there?" I pointed toward a spot where I would be sitting behind Henry and could still see past him.

The harem girl—I could see now that she was wearing a bright metal slave collar at her throat, and it made me wonder how these places had changed since I'd been young enough to actually want to go in one—guided me through the maze of empty tables and chairs to the area I had selected. I was almost disappointed that she didn't drop down and prostrate herself at my feet before she left. She just showed me a chair and was gone before I realized she was leaving.

A dark-haired harem girl materialized to take the first one's place, and by way of the lip-to-ear routine we established that a Coors Light would slake my desires for the moment. She was very quick and efficient in serving it. She also charged me two bucks for the damn thing. I'll bet the owner of this place was a happy man.

I laid my cigarettes and lighter down, positioned the ashtray exactly where I wanted it, took a sip of the bright, clear brew, and settled down to my duties.

The sinuous, bumping-and-grinding body of that leggy redhead on the runway, the one with nothing but body jewelry in the way of clothing to decorate that trim, writhing figure—she wasn't going to distract me in the least from my task of keeping an eye on ol' Henry Blair. Nossir, she wasn't.

15

Henry Blair seemed to be a simple enough man in his evening tastes. Simpleminded, even. Uncomplicated. I still couldn't understand him. Nor the other leering fellows who shared his fascination with the girls of the Cat's Meow.

Don't get me wrong. The girls were pretty enough. Young, with the tautness of muscle and smoothness of skin that that implies. Powdered and scented. Breasts well proportioned and barely sagging as yet. Flat of belly. Vaginal hair trimmed but not actually shaved, encouraging close inspection. One of them—they took turns dancing on the runway, each beginning her set of jukebox songs more or less clothed and dancing each successive number in a greater state of undress until the final selection was fully nude—had a Harley-Davidson tattoo over her right breast and a tiny honeybee tattooed in the fringes of her pubic hair.

The harem girls did not dance on the runway, but all of them, dancers and waitesses alike, were attractive enough to give a healthy man an erection.

But as far as I could see, there was no place for a fellow to go with his pulsing problem once he got that way.

Which is why I couldn't really figure these fellows out.

All they seemed to get for their money—and they spent quite a lot of it—was frustration.

I mean, I can understand a guy paying for the privilege of having a warm body to wrap his arms around and curl up close to. Which is what prostitution is all about anyhow. The ejaculation is only an excuse. That much you can get for free with your own right hand.

But these guys weren't getting that or anything close to it.

The girls came out onto the runway, and they bumped and ground, and they smiled down into the eyes of their stage-side customers, and the guys put folding-money tips out onto the edge of the runway like the bills were just so much confetti.

But all they got in return for those green-inked offerings was a close-up eyeful when the girl danced down into a squat to pick up the tips.

My gosh, having a pretty stranger's vaginal lips spread wide maybe six inches in front of their noses must have been what they wanted. But why? Why would these guys be wishing more frustration on themselves when they could look but not touch?

I found myself really wondering what the patrons were getting out of it.

The girls I could understand. They were getting paid for their labors, and paid darn well from what I could see.

It was no wonder there didn't seem to be any hooking going on in the place. A working girl turns tricks for money, not pleasure, and it was obvious that these gals were already making so much money they didn't need to take the risks of whoring to get more.

But the guys?

That I just couldn't understand.

Blair seemed to, though. He seemed to understand it all just fine.

The guy grinned and squirmed on his chair and sucked at his drink and leered at the girls and hollered out loud whenever one of them smiled at him, and poured his money out onto the edge of the runway just like the rest of them.

I shook my head. Couldn't figure it. Still can't. Probably never will.

Ol' Henry, though, enjoyed himself that way for a couple hours before he packed it in for the night.

Even then I was expecting something more after all that teasing, tantalizing buildup. At the least, I figured, these guys were gearing up for a shot at the streetwalkers who make their rounds in the sleazier districts of every GI town and every major city.

Maybe, I was thinking, the patrons of places like the Cat's Meow were working themselves up to some "real" action afterward.

Not so, I discovered. From the nude bar, old Henry went straight to his car and straight for home, which turned out to be an apartment in a converted grand old house near the downtown district.

The apartment, I couldn't say much about, since he didn't invite me inside, but the house had gone to seed after its onetime glory. I doubted that the apartment would have been any better, in spite of Blair's fine car and the free way he tossed his money onto that runway.

The guy definitely was not filled with couth.

I sat outside in my rental chariot and watched lights go on in some second-floor rooms after Henry entered the place. A few minutes later the lights went out again, not even leaving a telltale glow from a television screen.

This, apparently, was the extent of Henry Blair's existence. Punch out on the time clock, McDonald's to satisfy the inner man, then a few drinks and a period of leching with the eyes only at girls he would never get to touch. Then home and off to an empty bed. The life seemed even emptier than the bed must have been.

I gave it up for the night and drove back to reclaim my Jeep.

I found that I was feeling sad for myself and for all the Henry Blairs of the world as I drove through the thinning evening traffic.

I was also feeling horny. It's a shame we can't all be satisfied as easily as Blair and his buddies back at that joint.

16

"Where have you been lately, Carl? Junior tells me you haven't been at the plant very much." Alexandra Goodroe was an enormously attractive girl even over the breakfast table. And there aren't all that many who can meet that test.

On the other hand, I didn't trust her worth a damn. I had been pretty much expecting exactly this question—if I had any reason to be suspicious of her anyway—and now here it was. I smiled at her across the soft-boiled eggs and toast she had prepared just the way I like them.

"I've been goofing off on your dad, actually. My Beemer got torn up a few months ago. It's in the junk heaps now. I've been looking for a replacement."

"Beemer? That sounds like a piece of construction equipment," she said.

"Motorcycle," I said. "BMW. Very classy. They're made by the same people that make the classy cars, but the bikes are more fun."

She smiled and pretended to be interested. "I've always wanted to ride a motorcycle, but Daddy wouldn't let me when I was little, and I don't know anyone who has one now. Did you, uh, have a wreck with yours or something?"

"Something like that." I went on eating my eggs. I didn't want to go into any details on the subject. Aside from the fact that it was still a painful subject, talking about attempts on one's life is not a socially acceptable form of breakfast conversation. And I didn't want to give her any ideas in that direction.

"Are you a safe driver, Carl?"

"I think so. And it's rider, not driver. You drive a car but ride a horse or a bike." I finished the eggs and reached

75

for the ashtray for a welcome after-meal smoke. A filthy but thoroughly enjoyable habit.

"Are you going to go look at a motorcycle today?"

"Probably."

"Could I come with you?" She was smiling oh so sweetly. You know. The kind wherein butter wouldn't melt.

I couldn't quite decide if this pretty but treacherous lass was trying to get a rise out of me or was just trying to throw off my schedule. Since I didn't have any particular schedule to keep, and since I could find good old Henry Blair any quitting time that I wanted him, the answer was an obvious one. "Come along," I told her. I tried to make myself sound cheerfully eager for her company.

Her pop had long since headed for the plant, and Junior had not yet made his bleary-eyed morning appearance, so I helped her with the dishes and then held the door for her to join me in the Jeep. She was smiling the whole way. Gee, wasn't this fun.

Actually, of course, there are few things I do enjoy more than cruising Motorcycle Row along Academy Boulevard. It almost makes me understand how a woman must feel when she is turned loose in a jewelry store. All those glittering, gleaming, lovely things lined up to look at and ooh upon.

The market has gotten so competitive lately, what with the economy craze and all, that you can find more to choose from in any given shop today than you could in the whole streetful of them a few years ago.

Flashbikes of the grunt-and-growl syndrome are out of favor lately, but the mid-sized machines are quicker today than the superbikes were just a few years ago and handle better than GP racers used to. It's an amazement, particularly the trend to turbocharging. Nearly everybody offers at least one turbo model now, and most of them are styled to make a grown man's mouth water. I know they're enough to make me daydream of pulling Kenny Roberts on a sweeper or beating Mamola out of Turn 9.

So I damn sure didn't mind spending a day in solid admiration.

We talked to Tom at the Yamaha shop and Roger at

Kawasaki and Wally at Honda. All of them have turbos to show off. Prettier than diamonds any old day.

Unfortunately, and in this case I can understand it, the check rides come only after you've put your money down. And I wasn't sure yet that a turbo was the way I wanted to go for my next canyon strafer. I've heard too many war stories about guys who get onto the throttle in the middle of a corner, just the way they've always done, and go splashing over the guardrails when that boost kicks in like an afterburner. Turbos are indisputably awesome, but I wanted to read a few more magazine reports before I made up my mind about them.

Sandy didn't seem to mind. She admired everything and sat on them and pretended delight with the whole business of window-shopping. I noticed that she was choosing to sit—making a hinting suggestion by it?—in the passenger's position on the showroom models.

Since I was already in the neighborhood I figured I might as well do some serious looking too, so we dropped in on Doc at the BMW shop. He greeted me by name.

"Are you ready yet?"

I shook my head. "Not quite." I sighed. There is something about the RS with that smooth, smooth fairing and those factory rearsets and low bars that just makes me quiver. Especially since they're coming stock with Krauser bags these days. A fella wouldn't have to add a thing before taking off for a look at the ocean waves.

"I have a demo outside," he offered.

"You're on." I didn't feel any qualms about enjoying one of his machines for a few hours. Not here. Hard sell isn't necessary with a Beemer. People ride them because they love them, and once they have one they'll probably be back for another. The Japanese techno-freaks summon you in with glitter. BMW holds you with quality.

Anyway, we borrowed a couple helmets, let the sleek beastie get its innards warm, and went for a leisurely run up Ute Pass. All climbing curves, that is a drive that never fails to give my insides a glow of pleasure, and it damn sure felt good to be on two wheels again after so long.

The day had turned warm, and the RS fairing sliced through the air and we whispered quickly past crusty

snowbanks on the north slopes as we climbed. It all felt so
fine I forgot my animosities for the girl who was riding
pillion behind me.

We hit Woodland Park and pulled in at the Godmother's
for a cup of coffee before starting back down again. Sandy
was grinning broadly when she dismounted. She pulled her
helmet off, and that medium-brown hair spilled out to
catch the sunlight. Damn she looked nice.

"That was *fun*," she squealed.

"I noticed you weren't hanging on so tight after the first
couple minutes."

"It was really comfortable. I couldn't believe it. How
fast were we going?"

I grinned and held a finger over my lips. "Shhhh."

"Well, anyway, I loved it."

"That's what counts."

Over coffee in the tiny cubicle beyond the main dining
area Sandy was waxing ecstatic about the pleasures of the
riding. "Do you think I could handle one myself?"

"Of course. They build little bitty ones for five-year-
olds. You wouldn't want to start with a thousand like that
RS out there, but there are some awfully good bikes you
could try. The Kaw . . ." I realized what I was about to
say and shut my mouth.

Once upon a time, not so very damned long ago, I had
known a lady who rode a little Kawasaki. It was my damn
fault that she was dead now. My stupid fault.

I think what I felt the most guilty about now was that it
had been so long since I had thought about her.

That seemed like even more of a betrayal.

I guess my poker face was not in place. "What's wrong,
Carl? Did I say something wrong?"

I shook my head.

"Something to do with small bikes? A ladyfriend,
maybe?" She reached across the table and touched my
wrist.

I glared at her. She had no damned right to be so
perceptive. Didn't she know that the guys in the black hats
aren't supposed to be sensitive to the feelings of others?
And she was a bad guy, behind whatever was wrong at her

own father's plant, wasn't she? Wasn't that what this whole spying day was all about?

I grunted. I didn't want to get to liking the damn woman anyway. So this was working out just fine. I'd just needed a little reminder there. Reminders about several things, maybe. I should have been grateful to her instead of angry.

"We better go back now," I said.

We rode back down the pass in silence, and this time there were no squeals or grins when we got off the RS. I returned the handsome bike and took Sandy home in the unexciting Jeep.

My mood could have been a whole lot better than it was.

17

Blair said something, and the dancer—I really hadn't decided yet if between sets they were actually hustling drinks or just encouraging the customers to snort the stuff down—leaned over to listen to him over the mad cacophony of what passed for music in here.

The girl was sure enough giving him an eyeful. Down off the stage she was wearing a sequined G-string and a scarf draped around her neck. She had a high-rise chest that brushed lightly over Blair's shoulder when she bent down to him. That didn't seem to make him mad.

He said something fairly lengthy, and one sly hand slid around the girl's powdered hip to cop a light feel. She evaded it deftly, without losing her professional smile.

Whatever the question, and I could guess what it must have been, he got a negative shake of the head in return. But the girl was still smiling. I've always said, there's nothing like a pro, whatever the field of endeavor. This gal was definitely a pro.

She went away, and Henry went back to his drink and to a close inspection of the girl who was dancing onstage at the moment. It was the girl with the Harley tattoo. After three nights running in this same bar and nothing to go home to but a sheet and a pillow, I was close to sending in an application to join a friendly local outlaw biker gang if it would mean getting close to something warm.

Really, though, I was getting kind of bored with this stuff about solitary drinking and nocturnal frustrations. Enough was more than enough, but I sure hadn't learned much yet about Blair beyond this one personal quirk. I sighed and took another swallow of my third Coors of the night.

Blair managed to tear his eyes away from the dancing outlaw gal long enough to get up and head for the men's room. He stumbled on the way there, although I didn't think he had been drinking enough to get in that kind of condition. Certainly he had had more than that the other nights I'd been watching him, and I hadn't seen him drunk yet. Maybe this was my big opportunity. I always love watching drunks. You bet.

It was earlier than he usually left the place, but when he came back into view he got his jacket from his chair, tossed down a tip that folded and was made up of several pieces—he sure was free with his money here for a man on a delivery driver's salary—and headed for the door.

I gave him a moment to get clear and followed.

"How 'bout that," Blair said happily as I cleared the door into the crisp night air. He was waiting for me. And he sure didn't look anything close to drunk now.

I grinned at him. "Good evening."

"I seen you watching me. Didn't recognize you at first," he said.

"At least we aren't going to have to pretend we never met before," I told him.

Blair laughed. "I know you well enough, man. Well enough to whip your ass a second time."

"Are you getting paid for this one too?"

"It's going to be my pleasure, man. My pleasure."

A customer came around the corner of the building from the parking lot and pushed between us to reach the door. The music was loud while the door was open. When it swung shut again there was still the thumping reverbera-tion of the rock beat coming through the walls. Blair stepped politely aside for the guy to pass, but he kept his eyes narrowed and locked firmly onto me. I got the impres-sion he thought I might want to get away from him. I didn't.

"Shall we go around back where we won't be bothered by strangers, Henry?"

His eyes widened a little when I used his name. "After you, man."

I chuckled a bit. "As I recall, Henry, you've been behind me once before. I hate to say this about a fella I hardly know, Henry, but I don't believe that you are entirely trustworthy. Why don't we walk around there together?''

Blair grunted and sidled around the side of the Cat's Meow toward the shadowy area behind the building. He was watching me, and I was watching him just as hard. No, I wasn't going to turn my back on the bastard a second time.

Wasn't going to trust him to play by the Marquess of Queensberry rules, either.

Blair reached a patch of deep shadow, planted his foot in the middle of a seemingly normal stride, and spun around with a real haymaker that was armed and dangerous.

If I hadn't been expecting something of the sort it would have plucked my head clean off my shoulders. Which was exactly what old Henry was wanting.

I bobbed to the left to let the punch pull him off balance, stepped inside it, and popped him a quick combination over the kidney.

It felt like hitting one of those slabs of hanging beef in *Rocky*. I wasn't sure that I hadn't hurt myself more than I did him. Mr. Blair was in excellent condition indeed.

He whipped his fist around in a backhanded swat that was another attempt to remove my valued head, but I wasn't entirely ignorant of that possibility either. I didn't happen to be there at the same time his hand was.

"Take your time, Henry. We have all night," I advised him.

The man did not seem to place much value on my suggestion. He cussed me enough to start a whole new fight and began bobbing and weaving the way a talented amateur boxer will.

"Had yourself some lessons in the manly art, Henry? Let me give you another." I stepped in closer and began to bob and weave right along with him. That made him mad, and he cussed me some more.

"You have a foul mouth, Henry. You could get a fella riled saying things like that."

He cussed me all the more. In mid-word he jabbed a couple feints and let fly with his big punch again.

This time I ducked the other way, stepped into him

buckle to buckle, and ripped a hard left low in the gut where a referee would have gotten all over me hollering foul. We weren't playing by the rules here, though.

I paid for it with a glancing shot over my ear and got a reminder from that that Blair was quick and could damn sure punch. I danced back out of the way and watched him go through his dance routine again.

By this time I was pretty sure Blair had done some ring work, amateur or maybe club-level stuff. Certainly he was moving and jabbing the way a prizefighter will. He was much more of a fighter than a brawler anyway. It gave me an idea.

"Come on, Henry. Put 'em up. That's the way, boy. Let's go at it, now. Yeah. Jab. Jab. Now the cross."

I called them as they came in and blocked them with a flurry of wrists and forearms, and every time I did, it made him madder and madder. He was getting really pissed off.

Mad enough to try a most unscientific haymaker again. He reared back like Gaylord Perry setting up to fling a fast ball and let 'er rip. I wasn't anywhere around by the time it traveled all that distance, and he swung himself halfway around with the force of it. I stepped in and gave his kidneys another greeting.

"Careful now, Henry. You're fixing to lose your cool. They warned you about that."

Neither of us was hurt in any way, but you couldn't hardly tell that from looking at Henry. He was puffing and glaring and red in the face. It was all from anger and exertion, of course, but it was getting him to where I wanted him to be. I really don't like folks who try to put dents in my skull from behind.

"Try again, Henry," I taunted him.

The silly bastard was so mad now he had forgotten everything he had ever learned. He lowered his guard and balled his fists the way a junior-high-school kid fights.

He let out a wordless bawl of frustrated anger and charged straight for me.

Me, I wasn't either scientific or fair about any of it. I stood watching him come into range and then punted him square in the cods.

There's a lot to be said for the pointy toes on good old Justin boots, by gum.

Blair went dead white in the face and dropped to the ground before all the air had time to swoosh out of his lungs. He didn't have enough left to yell with, and he curled into a ball like an armadillo with a dog on its tail.

I wasn't sure that anybody was going to straighten Henry Blair out with anything less than a block and tackle for the next little while.

I squatted down beside him and said, "It hurts, don't it Henry?" I was grinning at him.

His eyes were working, but that was about all he was interested in moving at the moment. That was enough. There was enough hate in them to tell me he'd been repaid in full.

His mouth worked, but nothing came out. It was just as well. If he'd said any of what he was wanting to say, it might have made me mad, and he wasn't in much of a position to want another round right now.

"Let me know when you're brave enough to try me again, Henry." I lighted a cigarette and made damn sure that the adrenaline rush that was keeping me pumped up didn't show in a shaking hand. "Have yourself a nice day, Henry," I said.

I got the hell out of there before somebody saw us and called the cops.

18

Henry Blair did not go to work the next day—which was hardly cause for amazement—and as far as I could tell no one came in to sympathize with him in his pain. Certainly no one that I could spot.

Really I had been more than half-expecting to see Alexandra Goodroe offer some nursing assistance, though I wasn't prepared yet to guess just how personal her concern would have been.

I think I was shying away from that subject on the grounds that in spite of everything, Sandy Goodroe was an awfully nice-looking girl. And Henry Blair was simply awful. A creep of the first water, however well built. Somehow I just didn't want to develop visions of a nice-looking girl like that being dumb enough to go for a wad of ignorant muscle like Blair seemed to be.

That is a curious thing about us humans. We tend to idealize the attractive. A pretty woman can be just as much of a slut as a scag, but we don't like to think so.

Hell, the physically attractive kids both male and female get superior grades in their school years and advance higher and faster in their later jobs than their plainer counterparts will, even when things like intelligence are dead even with those plainer competitors. Simple human nature. And I knew it. And even knowing it, I found myself falling into the same trap of judgment.

Anyway, I plain and simple did not want to think about Sandy Goodroe having that kind of connection with Henry Blair. A connection, sure—that I was willing to buy. But not on a personal level. Just greed and larceny and forgivable stuff like that.

So I sat at a considerable distance from the Blair apartment and wasted the day away.

One thing was for certain sure. This close-range surveillance was out of the question now as far as Henry Blair
was concerned. He was expecting me now, with beard and
without, and from here on if I wanted to keep an eye on
the gentleman it was going to be with great care.

Somehow I didn't believe he was thinking kind thoughts
about me today, and it would probably be prudent for me
to make damn sure he never got a second chance to get
behind my back with a club or a rock or an antitank gun. He
probably would be happy to use any of them on me now.

So now I was carrying a set of ten-power glasses and a
great deal of caution.

Blair didn't show his nose outside his apartment at all
that day, so I really had not accomplished much when I
called it quits and headed back to the Goodroe house in the
evening.

Dinner was already on the table when I walked in.

Glen was on his feet with a handshake and a greeting
and a smile on his face. "We thought you weren't going to
make it, Carl. Sandy—"

She was already bringing another place setting for me.
"I told Daddy you were probably looking at motorcycles
again and lost track of the time."

She certainly seemed friendly enough. I wondered if she
had not yet heard about the little accident Mr. Blair suffered.

Junior was at the table, but he seemed preoccupied with
something this evening. He was already loading his plate
while his sister and Glen were fussing around to get me
settled with them, and I don't think Junior said half a
dozen words during the whole meal. Something was bothering him. Probably his computerized games, I figured. He
took that stuff awfully seriously.

Sandy chattered through the meal for a change—usually
she was the one who was disapprovingly silent—and Glen
benignly presided over the meal, smiling and nodding and
contributing a word here and there, although he too seemed
preoccupied.

After dinner Junior disappeared into the cold night air
and Glen asked me to join him in the family room.

"Yes, Glen?"

He sighed. Heavily, I thought. "Are you making any progress, Carl? Any progress at all?"

"I . . . Damn little if any, Glen. I wish I could give you a better answer than that, but I can't." I didn't want to go any further than that. After all, I didn't *know* a damn thing so far. All of it was guesswork. And I sure didn't want to throw guesses at him that would involve his own cherished daughter. He had enough on his shoulders without that. "Is there a reason you asked?"

He nodded. "I'm so close, Carl. So close to breaking through with the Rainbow Drive. If anyone gets hold of my new patent drawings now,"—he shrugged—"it would be disastrous at this point." He stood and crossed the room to stare out the window, although I doubt that he saw anything out there.

"At this point of the development, Carl, I should be as excited as a child on Christmas Eve. I really should be. I know exactly where I want to go with it now. I know just how I want to do it. All I have to do is to finish the mechanical details of the drawings. Strictly undergrad stuff, anyone could do it. All of the real work has already been done and is tucked away in my head. But dammit, Carl, once I put it on paper it is vulnerable. It can be stolen then. Once I put it down on paper, any common thief can walk out with it, and the Rainbow Drive would belong to the highest bidder."

No wonder he seemed concerned. And the poor guy was right. If he had solved the problems of the design and was ready to apply for patents, this right now should have been the joy-making time. The time to celebrate and break open the champagne and have a loud office party and let down from the tensions of creative work.

He couldn't do that. He was afraid to.

"Do you have the research room secure?" I asked.

Glen nodded. "I put a guard on it today. I . . . It really hurt me to do it. It hurt some feelings around the shop too, I'm sure. I brought some people in from outside the organization, and from now on I'm the only one who goes in there. God, I hated to do that. I just didn't know what else I could do."

"That's what I would have suggested, though, Glen."

"I guess it had to be done." He turned from the window and began to pace around the room. "You saw how upset Junior was this evening."

I nodded.

"I hurt his feelings today. My own son, Carl. The guards wouldn't even let him inside. I had some tables in there that he needed for his project, and they wouldn't let my own son in to look at them because I left orders that no one be allowed through." He looked at me, and there was a deep unhappiness in his eyes. "My own son, Carl."

"Don't worry about it, Glen. You got the tables for him, didn't you?"

"I wasn't there at the time. I can give them to him tomorrow, of course, but the damage has already been done. Those guards were acting on my orders, and I never thought to tell them he could go in. I just never thought to tell them that."

"He'll get over it. We all get mad and we all get glad again. It's no big deal." Big comfort, I know, but hell, fathers and sons get into fusses all the time.

"Daddy?" Sandy was at the door, apparently through with her cleanup chores. I wonder if she had been listening to any of this before she spoke.

"Yes, honey?"

"I wondered if you and Carl would like a drink after dinner."

Glen shrugged.

"That probably would be a good idea," I said. "Your pop is feeling down on himself this evening."

She looked concerned. If she was playacting, she was doing an awfully fine job of it. "What is it, Daddy?"

He shook his head. "Nothing really." He brightened. "But I think I would like a cocktail."

She mixed three somethings that I didn't bother to inquire about. It was something sweet, which killed it as far as I was concerned, but it wasn't poisonous so I figured I could drink it like a little man.

Goodroe seemed to relax a little with the girl in the room. It was pretty obvious that he took pride in his daughter. He seemed to actually like her company.

"Did you have a good day, honey?"

She smiled. "The usual. You know. Bonbons in front of the TV. The mad social whirl of grocery shopping. Like that."

Glen laughed. To me he said, "Sandy is notorious for her grocery shopping. She goes just about every day. Or is it *every* day now?"

She made a face at him. "That isn't fair. Often, yes. Daily, no."

"Did you lock yourself out of the truck today?"

"Daddy!" The squeal had a lot of embarrassment in it. Sort of like when Mom and Pop drag out the bearskin-rug pix to show the first boyfriend.

Goodroe was enjoying the opportunity to tease her. "Did she tell you about that, Carl? No, I'll bet she didn't, by Godfrey."

"Daddy, don't."

He ignored the pleading. "The other day she went to the grocery and locked herself out of her truck. I had to have the courier take my keys to her before she could get home."

"Courier?" I asked stupidly.

Glen was still laughing at his daughter's squirms. "The people we use to ship our program tapes. He has to go right by there and he was at the plant at the time, so I asked the driver to drop them off on his way by. Nice people, actually. Very pleasant to do business with. Why do you ask?"

"I . . ." I had egg on my face. I shook my head. "The question just popped into mind, that's all. Sorry."

Glen shrugged.

Sandy didn't seem to think anything about it either.

But if Henry Blair met Sandy Goodroe in that parking lot to deliver a set of car keys from her dad . . . *then who the hell was his connection at G&G Electronics?*

I was back to square one and couldn't even apologize to Sandy for the things I had been accusing her of in my guesswork.

Damn!

19

I had been thinking right along that Sandy Goodroe was the fly in her father's ointment, but now it seemed I was going to have to start from scratch again.

It still came back to the question of who might have known that I was going to be in that restaurant parking lot the night Henry and his pal jumped me.

There was a trap I had to watch out for there, of course. Sandy still was one of the people who had known. I couldn't afford to mark her off my list of possibles just because it turned out I was wrong about her contact with Henry Blair.

On the other hand, I was right back to the fact that anyone at G&G Electronics might have known. Might. That was the key word.

And at this point, after so much time had passed, there was small chance that I could go nosing around to find out. Even I couldn't remember who all might have overheard my conversation with the receptionist that afternoon when I was expecting to say good-bye to Glen. If I couldn't remember myself, I sure couldn't expect any uninvolved employees at the company to remember it for me.

I did a lot of headshaking and pondering in the privacy of my borrowed bed that night. I also kept finding myself wanting to believe that Sandy Goodroe was no part of it.

Part of that, of course, was an attempt to absolve myself of guilt for having falsely accused her in the Blair meeting. Part of it was just because she was such a pretty girl. was, I admit, attracted to her. Therefore I didn't want her to be guilty of anything remotely wrong. Illogical? Sure. But it was so.

I gave up worrying about it and went to sleep knowing

that at least I still did have that one solid lead, Mr. Blair. He was definitely tied in to it, even if I had no idea with or through whom. Him I didn't suspect, him I knew damn good and well about.

Henry Blair might not have been well enough to go to work after his little accident at the Cat's Meow, but he wasn't going to let a few aches and pains ruin his weekend.

The man was a fast-food junkie for most or possibly all of his meals. At least I never did see him buy any groceries unless you count chips and dips from a convenience market as grocery shopping. Breakfasts and suppers were at McDonald's, lunch was courtesy of Wendy's. Regular as could be. I don't have anything against either place, like them right well myself from time to time, but day after day of the same thing would have driven me plumb off the idea of eating. Blair didn't seem to mind it in the least.

Friday evening he spent back in the Cat's Meow. This time he went inside alone, though, since I wasn't going to take the chance of letting him know I was still watching him. I stayed outside and kept an eye on the place from long range.

I was figuring that he probably was letting the first meeting go—on the theory that he had jumped me and I was getting some revenge for it. A second time, after I'd already whipped him for that, would have to be a deliberate tail trying to point to whoever put him on me. And I didn't want him telling that tale to anyone else, or my chances would be blown, probably forever. This time I had to be genuinely careful not to be seen.

Besides, I didn't need any more of the frustrations that come from frequenting joints like that one. I could watch just as happily from outside the damn place.

Saturday night, after the obligatory visit to the Golden Arches, Henry broke his pattern and went to a different bar.

This one was not in the Meow mold. No signs promising nude dancers or taxi dancing, which some of those places are getting back to. Just a rather sleazy-looking bar on South Tejon with the usual lighted window displays promising Coors and Bud and poor confused Marv's favorite brand.

The place did seem to have one other rather obvious attraction, though, and I guessed that old Henry was about to get rid of a week's frustrations from the Cat's Meow.

The street-side parking slots near the place were filled with the usual assortment of GI junkers and pickup trucks, but down at the end of the block there was a separate section that by common consent seemed to be reserved for a flock of highly polished Lincolns and Caddies.

The occupants from those cars, at least the males who got out of them, wore loud clothing and weird hats. Out here you get used to seeing wide-brimmed cowpoke hats on even the most dignified businessmen, and billed caps bearing logos for feed dealers and grain elevators and construction companies are about as common.

These guys were duded up in feathered rigs straight off the old Rooster character in the *Baretta* television series.

I mean, if they wanted to advertise the fact that they were pimps, they had chosen a pretty fair way to go about it.

I glassed them from a distance and passed some time daydreaming about how much fun it would be to wade into the whole stinking pile of them with a couple good old boys at my back. Or just with a baseball bat in my hands and forget the good old boys.

There is something about a pimp that pisses me off. Probably the idea that it is a form of slavery that has never gone out of style and that no one seems to give a damn about. It just goes on and on, and these creeps just get richer and richer. And more brazen about their bloodsucking.

That's all they are. A bunch of fucking leeches. And I'd stomp one of their heads as quick as I'd stomp on a leech.

Bastards. It made me mad just looking at them.

But that wasn't what I was here for, and I dragged myself back to the business at hand, hard as it was to ignore those crumbs down at the other end of the block.

The girls who got out of the cars and scattered onto the street—usually a pair to a car, though occasionally just one or sometimes three—were almost as obvious about how they earned their living.

The hookers came in a broad—no pun intended—assortment. From pudgy and middle-aged to hard-looking hussies in their mid-twenties to a few who were very young and very slim and actually right attractive. I understand that this wasn't the right area to find the really young kids who were hooking for drug money, that was farther uptown, but some of them were a lot younger than I expected to see in a street pimp's stable. Still, I guess there must be such a glut of supply that even some of the good-lookers were being turned for the GI trade.

Despite the fall weather that carries a chilling bite in the wind, most of them were decked out in hot pants and micromini-skirts—current fashion doesn't seem to be able to compete with the idea of a show of leg to act as a club between the prospective john's eyes—and fluffy fake-fur coats.

No purses, I noticed. But then, what would they need those for? The pimps would take care of the cash involved in their transactions. Of course they wouldn't need purses. Besides, that would only be something to risk leaving behind if they had to make a run from a cop or a nasty customer.

Looking into some of those blank faces, I was willing to bet that most of these girls would be able to take damn good care of themselves in a scrap, though. I'd have been glad to stand up to any or all of the pimps, but I wasn't sure that it wouldn't be wiser to run like hell if a bunch of those whores came after me with blood in their eyes.

The rules of the game seemed to be that the girls weren't to loiter in one spot too long.

They drifted into and out of the bar where Blair had disappeared, or they strolled around and around the block while they waited to be picked up.

Another rule seemed to be that they weren't to call out to the guys cruising past in their junk-heap cars. The girls would smile and wave but they wouldn't speak without being spoken to first.

Probably an entrapment dodge of some kind against prowling plainclothes cops, I figured. There are some pretty damned strange entrapment rulings these days, and this crowd would know a whole bunch more about them than I ever will.

The guys, entire carloads of GI's at a time or older

single men in a vehicle—"single" indicating only one guy in the car, not marital status, which I wasn't at all sure about—would stop. The gal would come over to the car window, and there would be some conversation, sometimes fairly lengthy.

Negotiations, I figured. I have no idea what the going rate is these days for a streetwalker, but judging from what I was watching I would say that it must be a negotiable figure that took a while to agree on.

Then the girl would either switch off the smiles and walk away stone-faced or would give a show of great joy and get into the car with the guy or guys.

The next time I hear or read some crap about a whore with a heart of gold, I'm going to remind myself of this experience. Watching the expressions of these gals after they failed to make a buck off a guy would be enough to cure anyone of fancy, romantic notions about street whores. As often as not, when they failed to hook a guy they gave him the finger and looked like snake venom come to life.

Anyway, I waited there for a while—longer than I expected to, actually—and after a time my buddy Henry came sauntering out of the joint with a hooker on his arm.

I can't say much for the guy's taste, unless he regarded this as a budget item to be tightly watched and was doing his shopping in the bargain basement. The broad was a dumpy-looking thing of at least forty and had to cake herself thick with powder to look *that* young. Maybe she had some special talents that didn't show. Not that it was any of my business.

They left in Henry's car, and I watched them drive out of sight. Wherever that ol' gal chose to do her business, I certainly had no interest. And I've never been much for peeping.

On the other hand, there was always the possibility, however slight, that the old boy might have been meeting someone there. I could understand the simple notion that he might just want to get it off. But still, this was a clear break from the routine I had seen him go through until now. Anyway, I wanted a look inside that joint just to see if I recognized any G&G employees.

It was only a short hike to the bar.

20

The place was a dive in the fine old tradition of all sleaze dives. Mirrors small and easily replaceable, glassware tucked carefully out of sight beneath the bar, bowls of stale—I tried them—pretzels and popcorn along the unpolished surface of the bar, a pervading odor of spilled beer and dribbled urine and ancient cigars long since disintegrated into dust in the cracks of the floor. A joint, pure and simple.

The customers included a few pimps, a few poorly dressed civilians, and a few wistful-looking soldiers in civilian clothing. I still don't understand how it is so easy to distinguish an eighteen-year-old GI in civvies from an eighteen-year-old UCCS student, but it is a fact that it can be done and no one seems to have any trouble doing it.

A trio of gaudily rouged whores were resting their feet and nursing beers at one of the tables near the front door. I got a quick sweep with three pairs of dull eyes when I first came through the door and then they turned away and went back to staring into the sudsless stuff in their glasses. That was neither encouraging nor flattering and I began to wonder what the hell was wrong with me if I couldn't even get a rise from a hooker.

Talk about instant depression . . . I didn't even have to add water.

The joint had a narrow street frontage, but ran deep, and the low-wattage bulbs over the bar could not begin to reach the back of the place. The entire G&G staff could have been holding a meeting back there and I would not have known it until or unless my eyes adjusted.

The customers in joints like that are not normally my idea of good companionship, and besides, my granddad told me all about Wild Bill Hickok and Jack McCall. There are some places where I'm just not comfortable unless my back is against a wall. I headed for the back of the place.

I groped my way to the farthest table, resisted an impulse to flick my Bic, and found the back of a rickety bentwood chair by feel.

"Welcome."

I damn near came out of my skin and must have been pretty obvious about it, because the voice began to laugh. "I won't bite."

"Oh, I . . . didn't see you here. I'm sorry. Really."

"I already promised I wouldn't bite." The voice was feminine and friendly. And slightly amused at the moment.

I looked down and discovered that surprise had balled my hands into fists. I relaxed and let them drop.

"Join me?" There was a catch in her voice that made the question sound more hopeful than polite.

"Are you sure?"

"Please." There was that same hopeful urgency in the word. She really meant it. I sat.

My eyes were beginning to adjust to the gloom, and I could see a black-on-black shadow figure of long, dark hair and a pair of small hands folded on top of the table. There was no glass in front of her, just an ashtray on the tabletop. I was sure I had never seen her before, not at G&G or anywhere else. There was also no one else in the dark back end of the place. So Henry had not come here to meet anyone, just to do some business of the obvious kind.

To get a better look at the girl I was sitting with—such novelty, oh what a clever fellow I am—I lit a cigarette and allowed the lighter to burn a little longer than was necessary.

The overriding impression I got was of absolutely huge dark eyes set in a pale, thin face. Unhealthily pale and unhealthily thin, but the eyes very bright and very large and very dark. The hair was dark, dark brown and very long. She wore neither makeup nor jewelry, not even a barrette in her hair, and her navy-blue pullover shirt hung like it was on a wire hanger from narrow shoulders down to the level of the tabletop. She might be able to find work as a mannequin but never as a brick outhouse. Her face was pleasant in a plain sort of way, but I thought she might actually be attractive with some color in her cheeks and a touch of makeup around those eyes. Striking if not actually attractive.

"Not much to see, is there?"

"What?"

She laughed. "It's all right. I know what I am and I know what I'm not, and what I'm not is much to look at."

Caught, by gum, red-handed, but I made the standard protests anyway, and she was polite enough not to call me a liar.

A man of the approximate size and presumably the power of one of Fort Carson's medium tanks came to the table to glare at me. I assumed he was offering to take a drink order, although his grunting didn't specify.

"Coors for me," I said. I turned to the woman. "What would you like? Since you're nice enough to share your table."

"A glass of red wine, please. And"—she hesitated—"could we have a bowl of those pretzels too, please?"

The bartender grunted. His apron, I thought, did not make him look the least bit effeminate.

"You don't have to buy me anything, really," the girl said when he was gone.

"Only degenerates drink alone."

"Do you drink alone?" she asked.

"Sometimes."

"When you're done with your drink, would you like to fuck?"

I think I was more startled this time than I'd been when her voice came at me out of the darkness. And she asked it just as casually as if she'd been asking for a cigarette.

Somehow her use of that particular word did not fit at all with those dark, deep eyes. And in spite of where she was sitting, I sure had not taken this girl for a damned hooker.

Mostly to give myself some time to do some rethinking, I said, "Those working girls up front didn't seem to see me as a likely prospect. Why would you?"

She shrugged. "You don't fit with the clientele here, mister. They think you might be a cop."

"And you don't?"

"Mister, I really don't care. If you pay me, that's fine. If you bust me, that's okay too."

"That's an interesting attitude."

She shrugged again but did not choose to elaborate.

The barman brought our drinks before I could think of anything particularly wonderful to say. I took a sip of my beer—even a joint like this couldn't ruin the taste of a bottled Coors—and she took a hummingbird sip of her wine. Then, I noticed, she pounced on the stale pretzels with rather serious intent. The whole soggy bowl of them didn't last more than a minute or so.

"Thanks," she said when the last of them was gone.

I'm a pretty brilliant fellow when I put my mind to it. It began to occur to me that this girl was *hungry*. Which might well explain why a jail cell would be acceptable to her. They do feed you in there even if the accommodations are not up to AAA standards.

"Could I ask you a favor, mister?" She drained off the last of her wine.

"Sure."

"Could you walk me out of this place? No obligations, you understand. I'm not asking for that. But could you kind of walk me out the front door and down the block a little ways?"

It was a curious request, but what the hell. "Sure," I said again.

We got up and she took a firm grip on my arm with both hands. To the others in the place it must have looked right chummy and possessive. Which must have been her intention, I was beginning to realize. I put my arm around her shoulders and did some hugging on her the way I guessed a good lecher should. She wasn't very tall, and her head ended up somewhere around armpit level, but she gave me a grateful look that told me I was guessing right for a change.

"If there's a gauntlet to be run, girl, let's do it," I said.

21

"My gosh, did you see the way that creep with the Jimmy Cagney twitch was looking at you?" I shook my head. "I don't know what they've got against you, but if I were you *I* think I'd stay out of that place from now on."

"It's all right, mister. They won't jump you or anything." She smiled. "It's bad for business to go around beating on the johns, you know."

I wasn't particularly worried about what some scummy pimp might want to try with me. As a matter of fact it would make for an almost welcome diversion. You know, sublimate the sexual drives into aggression and all that. But I couldn't hardly try to explain that to a total stranger without coming on as some kind of macho blowhard. Besides, she was the one they had been throwing daggers at out of those bloodshot eyes. Damn but those crumbs had looked mean.

She turned left and led the way down the block away from the corner where the pimps liked to park their shiny luxury cruisers. Near the corner she stopped and gave me a quite genuine smile, definitely not the kind the working girls passed out to their customers and prospects.

"Thanks," she said. She held her hand out to shake.

"Leaving?"

She grinned and used both hands to pull the material of her shirt—damn thin material for such a brisk night—tight against her chest. She had all the fullness of figure of your average fourteen-year-old boy. "So I'm not your type. No big deal, mister. I'll find something before the night's over or my name ain't Calamity Jane. And I really do thank you for walking me out." She extended her hand again and this time I took it, but I held on to it instead of just shaking and letting go. She'd gone and gotten me curious now.

"Would you mind humoring me for a moment, then?"

She grinned again, and in the better light under the streetlamps I could see an impish quality in that thin face. "You want to know what a nice girl like me is doing in this business, right?"

"No." There is no surer way to hear a lie than to ask a hooker about her background, and I'm not quite stupid enough to not know that. "I was wondering about those guys back in the bar."

"Oh, them." She sounded uninterested now that she was out in the clean night air. "They hadn't known I was back in that corner, and once they found out, well, I figure I got enough of a handicap without them rearranging my nose over by an ear or something. That's all." She sure sounded casual about it.

"You're a free-lancer, is that it?"

She flashed that grin again. "See, I've always said that not all johns are stupid." She hooked a thumb toward the gum-chewer who was still dutifully tromping around and around the same city block. "Those pigs, they don't so much as own their own twats." I think I winced a little. I'm an old-fashioned boy at heart and never have accepted the idea that women have as much right as men to the use of cusswords.

"And you offend the system?"

"Something like that, yeah." She laughed.

I looked toward the ample rear end of the gum-chewer receding down the block, and I couldn't help saying, "That one doesn't look like she's missed very many meals lately."

My newfound friend shrugged. "You give a little, you get a little. Listen, mister, I don't mean to be ungrateful or anything, but I've got to go do some cruising, okay?" She took her hand back. Actually I hadn't realized I was still hanging on to it.

"Wait." I don't really know why I said that. Hadn't intended to. Didn't know I was going to until it was already out.

It's a funny thing. I had come down here with business-like intentions having nothing to do with skinny, hungry

would-be whores. Now I found myself standing on a
public street corner feeling personally involved with one of
them.

And I was feeling involved with this odd hooker's odd
life.

Strange. But what did it, I think, is that she kept switch-
ing roles from the crude ass-peddler to an almost innocent
waif and then back again. I couldn't quite figure her out.
And I guess I've always been a sucker for those hard-luck
tales that are seen but not told, the way good children were
once reputed to be.

Anyhow, I found myself clearing my throat. "Look,
you, uh, made an offer a while back."

"Yeah?"

"So I'd like to take you up on it."

She gave me a sad smile. "You don't have to do that,
mister."

I smiled back at her. "If you're going to bed down with
a stranger, it might as well be with somebody you like."
Damned if I didn't mean it, too. I did kind of like her.

"All right." She laughed. "I got some pride, but not so
much that I'll turn down an honest trick."

"One thing," I said.

A hint of worry flickered across her eyes, but she
covered it up quickly. "Yeah?"

"Before we . . . well, before. I'm kind of hungry.
Would you mind if we got something to eat first?" Actually I was still pretty well stuffed from the meal Sandy had
served back at the Goodroe homestead that night, but I
thought this odd, dark girl might be in real need of some
chow. And I wasn't in such a monumental hurry to abuse her
body that I couldn't wait while she got some nourishment.

"Whatever you want, mister." She tried to sound bored,
but she didn't carry that off very well. I felt sorry for her,
which I suppose is a blatantly patronizing, male-chauvinist-
pig sort of thing to do. But hell, I never claimed to be
anything but a country rube at heart. Besides, it was basis
enough for more of a relationship than a fellow ought to
expect when he goes out to pay for it.

I led her back up the block to my Jeep and helped her
into it. She accepted the gesture with ladylike grace.

I let the engine warm for a moment and ran down the possibilities of feeding her, deciding finally on one of those all-you-can-eat places halfway across town where the food is not Michelin Guide quality but where there is plenty of it. I had just come to that conclusion when I saw a man come out onto the sidewalk from an alley between the bar and a triple-X movie theater.

He paused for a moment to glance quickly left and right, then hurried into the crummy bar. If I had been parked at either end of the block, he would have spotted me for sure, but since I was sitting practically in front of him, he never saw me.

"What are you grinning about, mister?"

"Huh? Oh. I just saw a young friend of mine. I've wondered what he was up to when he disappears in the evenings. Now I know it's not video games. Not that I can blame him. I happen to be here too."

"Yeah." She slid low in the bucket seat and closed her eyes. "Come to think of it, I'm glad you're here, mister." She grinned. "Thank goodness all you men are beasts."

Her hand found my leg and unerringly ran up the inside of it to find the root of all man's problems. Well, some of man's problems. My response was instantaneous and damn near painful.

She laughed. "Are you sure you want to go eat?"

"I'm sure. I can wait that long anyway." Still, my reaction was more than I would have expected. I risked severe damage to engine and transmission getting to and from that eatery.

22

Oddly enough, I was still thinking about that darn girl the next day.

Not just the sex, although that was kinda fun to think back on too. I mean she might not have been built all that great, but she more than made up in imagination and vigor what she might have lacked in other areas.

What I kept thinking about, though, was—damn, I hate to admit it—what she was doing in that line of work.

All right. That's a mug's game. I *know* that. But I kept wondering just the same.

What it came down to, I guess, is that as a human being, as a person, she was not at all what I would have expected under those particular circumstances of occupation.

Stupid of me? Probably. But I found myself making up half a hundred different backgrounds for that girl, each of them plausible if only remotely so.

She was a perfectly nice, bright, ordinary girl-next-door type who ran away from home, against the advice of her family, with a handsome lover who turned out to be a creep. The guy ditched her and now she had too much pride to go crawling back to the familial hearthside.

She was a PK, a preacher's kid, who set off to show the world that she was no goody-goody and carried the scene too far. Now she had too much pride, etc.

She was a runaway years away from her home who had seen the California and the New Mexico scenes and been to and through and beyond the drug culture. Now she was drifting in search of a place to go and had too much pride . . . Haven't I done that bit already?

Funny. I kept coming back to the idea that basically she was a pretty nice, even decent kind of person.

I have no idea how much of that was her fault and how much of it might have been my own wishful thinking. But I do know that as a professional hooker that girl hadn't been very damn professional.

I mean, it was my understanding that a working girl always wants a complete program of events before the fact and a stiff fee negotiated on that basis. This gal hadn't even gotten around to mentioning money, and I hadn't thought of it myself until I was ready to leave the motel room I'd taken for the night.

When I did ask what she wanted for all she had done—and it had been considerable—she said offhandedly that twenty ought to do if that was all right with me. I'm not an expert on that subject, but the rate was far below what I expected and would have been willing to part with.

She accepted the twenty, and I doubled that as a sort of a tip and left the room key with her in case she wanted to do some more work that night.

But if she set out to confuse and intrigue me, she sure did a fine job of it, because afterward I kept wondering what the real deal was with her and whether she was eating and was okay. So I'm a chump first class; I don't deny it.

Anyway, I was still fretting about that little hooker and whatever her problems were. In fact, I pretty much convinced myself that the girl wasn't a whore at all but just a girl in critical need. And I'm a born sucker. Barnum would have loved me.

I got to thinking about that so much that I decided to find out what the going rates were down on South Tejon. I told myself that I was not, after all, going down there to look for the girl again. I just wanted to get a few more clues to her professionalism. You bet. The truth is that I didn't believe it either.

A few faces were different from the last time I had been there, but otherwise things seemed pretty much the same. A couple girls marched the pavement while the others waited their turn inside the bar. The pimps stood around drinking Southern Comfort and bragging to each other about how rich they all were.

I checked out the back corner of the bar, but there was

no familiar pale face in the darkness there. I'd been hoping there might be.

When you are lost, always make sure you are asking directions from somebody who knows how to get there. In this instance I figured that would be the bartender. He saw them all and ought to know every hooker who had ever worked the city. So I asked.

"I don't know what you're talking about, buddy."

"She was in here just last night," I protested. I described her.

The guy shook his head. "You're asking about a hoor, buddy. I don't know nothing about no hoors. They ain't allowed in here."

Right. I believed that, I did. I turned and pointedly looked toward the pair of them sitting by his front window with their wares on display. The guy remained totally wooden-faced.

Another law of human nature, I realized, belatedly understanding how stupid my question has been. The law is: Nobody knowingly rats on himself. This guy was no exception to the law.

"Thanks anyway," I said. I turned away and started out the front door.

"Hey, buddy."

"Yeah?" I turned back. One of the pimps was speaking to me.

Television has taught me that all pimps are tall and black and skinny and wear huge diamond rings and stickpins. This guy was white and beefy and wore hand-cobbled cowboy boots and a huge cowboy hat decorated with a good six pounds of feathers that had had a previous existence on the butt of a golden pheasant.

"C'mere." He beckoned me closer. With his other hand—turquoise, not diamonds in the several rings—he crooked a finger. A flat-bellied, high-breasted hooker with frizzy red hair materialized at his side within seconds. In addition to his other accomplishments the guy was a magician. I went over to see what it was he wanted to tell me.

"You want a little something, buddy, take Wanda here. She's as good as any you'll find. Clean kid, competitive rates. You'll be satisfied, I guarantee."

"I was looking for somebody in particular."

"That what I heard you telling Carl."

I looked toward the bartender. Thank goodness that lump of grumpy suet was no namesake of mine. "Yeah, well, I guess I'll keep looking. Thanks anyway."

"What I'm trying to tell you, buddy, is that you aren't gonna find Miss Priss."

"Oh?"

"She retired from the business, you understand."

"Really? Youthful retirement is a dream we all cherish." I knew before I said it that it would be lost on him. He looked like he had the intelligence of a field mouse. Sarcasm would never reach this yo-yo. "Tell me about it."

The pimp shrugged. "I don't know nothing about it myself, understand. I just heard tell. The point is, if you want some tonight, take old Wanda here." He reached down and took old Wanda by the left cheek and gave her a mighty squeeze. Her expression never changed.

"I'd rather hear more about Miss Priss," I told him. I was smiling. The very picture of a good old boy, all teeth and no brains.

"I told you all I know already, buddy. Take my word for it. Take Wanda or get the hell out of here. We ain't real fond of questions." He gave me a scowl that probably was supposed to send me into paroxysms of terror and rolled thick shoulder muscles. Somehow I forgot to be scared of him.

I was still smiling. "Tell me, buddy, did you rearrange her nose? Which ear did you leave it by? And more to the point, how many scumbags like you did it take to beat up on one skinny little girl? Three? Four? Half a dozen maybe?" I was grinning like a cat with feathers on its face. Damn, but I felt good. I shifted my weight onto my left foot.

"Look, buddy, I was tryin' to do you a favor. Don't come on smartass with me or you'll be hobbling at least a week. You know?"

"Actually . . . *buddy* . . . I don't think your kind is half man enough to teach me."

The pimp's right hand moved. I don't know where he intended for it to go, but it didn't go very far. My hand moved too, slicing almost straight up with the knuckles extended to make a dandy little cutting surface. It caught him under the chin and did wondrous things to the cartilage in his throat. He must have had his tongue kind of forward over his teeth at the time too, because there was an awful lot of blood coming out of his mouth.

Not that I had much time to stand and observe. His two pimp-pals were only feet away, and they took offense to the disrespect I was showing for their friend.

I heard the distinctive snick of a switchblade knife snapping open, and the nearer of them came for me hard and low.

Conveniently low.

He lunged at me fast, timing it to reach full extension as the blade entered my gut.

Normally that would be a devastatingly effective way to resolve a problem. Show a guy sudden and lethal violence and nine out of ten will stand in fascinated awe and watch the pretty steel disappear into their own midriff. I was not that fascinated and made it a point to move out of his way.

I skipped back a step and planted a boot on the bridge of the man's nose. Well, the girl last night had been concerned about the rearrangement of noses. Now it was their turn. The pimp went down, and I didn't think he was much interested in a second attempt.

The third one and the bartender were both poised like they were ready to do something drastic but were finding themselves suddenly unwilling.

"Like I said. Half a dozen at the very least." I smiled at them and bent to pick up the knife pimp number two was no longer holding.

"You boys don't want to take your shots? No? Well, I can't fault your judgment even if you do get low marks for bravery." I looked at the knife. It was one of those cheap jobs you can find for a few bucks in the Mexican border towns, theoretically illegal here, but the people who buy them aren't likely to declare them with customs. I flipped it toward the dirty linoleum of the floor, and since things were going so right for me, it landed perfectly and stuck upright with the point buried deep and the haft quivering nicely.

I backed out of there with a grin, actually hoping that either the remaining pimp or the bartender would take a run at me so I would have an excuse to nail him too. I didn't hurry. Didn't think there was very much likelihood that one of those cretins would call the cops.

Come to think of it, though, I never did find out what the going rate for commercial sex is on the streets these days.

But I figured that nice little free-lancer had gotten back at least some of her own, even if she never would know about it. That was something.

I cranked up my Jeep and went away.

23

On Sunday Junior was still in a pout, definitely no fun to be around, and Glen was down at the plant working on his drawings. Usually I thoroughly enjoy a Sunday afternoon of the NFL on the tube, but now it was a relief when Sandy asked if I'd like to go riding with her.

"You bet." Just that quick.

We piled the gear, an English saddle for her and a silver decorated show saddle for me, into the back of her little truck and took off for the countryside.

"Are you going to be out of luck when your dad gets his new plant built?" I asked as she drove.

She shook her head. I liked what that did to the sunlight in the gloss of her hair. "Daddy bought more than he really needs out there, so I can still fence off a piece of it." She grinned. "If he ever runs out of room on that site it would mean we'll be so rich from the Rainbow Drive that I could buy Penrose Stadium and keep them at the rodeo grounds with a full-time handler for each of them."

"Right." Penrose Stadium was county-owned and not likely to be sold, but I got the message.

Actually it is quite a nice setup for rodeos and horse shows and such. And there is already a public boarding stable there. Obviously not what she had in mind.

"Daddy said you used to do some rodeo riding," Sandy said. She kept her eyes on the road and talked into the windshield.

"A little. No big deal."

"Did you ever go to any of the rodeos at Penrose?"

"Sure. Little Britches when I was a kid. RCA later on."

"I thought it was the PRCA."

"It is. Professional Rodeo Cowboys Association nowadays. It used to be just RCA. And the Turtles Association 'way back before that, but please don't ask me why. I don't have the foggiest notion how they came up with that. That was back before I was born anyway."

"If I go over to the Hall will I find you there?"

"Not hardly. I was small potatoes, not like those boys." The PRCA headquarters and the Hall of Champions were just a few miles from where we were then, northeast of the Garden of the Gods. I never came close to being good enough to be listed in that exalted company.

Sandy seemed only mildly disappointed by my admission. She wheeled the Toyota into the drive, and this time I was feeling up to hopping out to open the gate.

The horses came to collect their tidbits, and she clipped the lead ropes onto them.

I let her tack up her own horse—she was perfectly capable at the chore and I am basically lazy anyway; there are times when women's lib comes in as a good excuse for behavior that would have been churlish just a few years ago—and she led the way out onto the road to the hills and woods that lay between the Interstate and the Black Forest area.

It's pretty country and it was a pretty day, and it felt damn good to be in some semiempty country again.

She stopped on top of a hill with a magnificent view of Pikes Peak and pulled some cheese and pepperoni out of her jacket pockets. "What do you think of it?"

"Nice."

"Is that all you have to say for it?" She looked practically insulted. She got down and dropped her reins to ground-tie the horse. That is a habit I've never had the courage to depend on, but hell, they were her horses. I stepped down and did the same thing. She handed me the sausage, and I broke a chunk off. The oily, garlic-laden flavor was good on the tongue, and a bite of cheese after it was cleansing.

"*Very* nice. Is that better?"

"What? Oh. I left that train of thought two minutes ago."

"What were you thinking of now?"

She gave me a small smile and a shrug and raised her face to the mountains. Her eyelashes were very long, I noticed, and her skin very finely textured. "I don't know that I could put it into words. I just . . . I was enjoying the day, I guess. Enjoying the ride. Riding in a ring is fun in its own way, but it can't compare with this. I just . . . like it."

"You don't have to explain. I know what you mean."

She looked at me, and I could see the enjoyment and the wonder of the open country in her eyes.

From here she could not reach it but she could see the start of it, and that was enough to give her some of the pleasure of it.

From where we stood we could see, almost hidden between us and the spectacle of the Peak, the carved red rock formations of the Garden of the Gods. "Right there," I said, pointing, "you can trailer your horses in and unload them. Climb up past that subdivision and on to Rampart Range Road. Once you cross the road, you can ride into some real country. Highway Sixty-seven is the only pavement between that subdivision and my ranch. It's glorious country up there, Sandy."

"You sound like that recommendation comes from memory instead of a map."

I sighed. "There isn't much of it that I haven't traveled." I grinned at her. "I'm working on what's left."

"Someday . . ." She stopped.

"Someday you might want to come with me. Once you cross my north fence you can go for weeks without seeing another soul if you want. Top out on one of those peaks and you can see the whole world spread out in front of you, from Denver down to New Mexico and west past the Collegiates and the Sangre de Cristos. It's something else."

We were quiet for a time. I know I was remembering and I suspect that she was imagining what it must be like, although there is no way the imagination can hope to meet the reality of the country that lay above us now. No way at all.

I felt a closeness with Sandy there in the thoughts that we were sharing. I felt drawn to her. It had nothing to do with the appetites that had been raised by a bunch of naked strangers in some damn bar. I am certain of that and made doubly certain of it in my own mind before I reached out to turn her and pull her closer.

Sandy's eyes were heavy-lidded and her lips parted slightly. She did not pull away. Her head lolled back, loose on the slim column of her neck.

I tasted her lips. Lightly at first and then with more insistence as the desire I was feeling for her grew and spread and brought an urgent stirring low in my belly.

The scent of her was delicate and very sweet. The taste of her breath in my mouth was just as sweet.

I felt her mold herself closer against me, and I allowed my arms to wrap her inside their circle.

My own breathing was becoming ragged, and I gently touched the incredible softness of her flesh along the smooth line of her jaw and beneath her ear.

Her hips pressed up and forward, and I stroked her back.

"No!"

Abruptly, with no warning at all, she was gone, twisting out of my arms and taking a few short, stumbling steps away. She was breathing very hard now—well, so was I—and her face was flushed with a warm hue that no cosmetic can ever hope to duplicate.

"No," she repeated.

"I . . ." I let the rest of it lie there unspoken. I didn't know what to say or how to attempt it.

She looked at me, and she looked angry—although with herself or with me, I could not have said.

I smiled at her, though it was not entirely an easy thing to do. I was having a little difficulty coming down from the place I had just been. "It's all right. I understand," I lied.

She still looked angry, but perhaps a little bit relieved now. "Are you sure?"

"Of course."

"You aren't angry?"

"No, of course I'm not angry." That much was the truth. Whatever her reason, the decision was hers to make, her right and her privilege. I guess I'd make a lousy masher and a worse lech.

THE VIDEO VANDAL

She definitely looked relieved now. She gave her shoulders a little twitch, the kind you make when a shiver runs up your spine, and I hoped that was a reaction to the arousal she had quite obviously been sharing with me and not some sort of reaction of repulsion to the idea of being kissed by a particular guy named Carl.

"I'm sorry," she said.

"It's all right." This time I meant it.

"Could we . . . ride back now?"

I gave her another smile, and this time it came easier. "Of course."

We didn't speak about it again, and I didn't touch her again. We rode back the way we had come, if at a slightly quicker pace this time, and by midafternoon we were back inside her father's fence.

I thought about warning her of the dangers—the stupidity, really—of leaving a horse to wander unattended with a halter on, but I didn't want to be the one to break the silence that was lying thick between us, and so let it go.

24

Monday morning Henry Blair went to work. Nothing particularly remarkable about that except that the crumb seemed to have changed jobs over the last couple days.

No more workingman's greens for old Henry. Now he was dressed in slacks and sport coat and even, by damn, a white shirt and tie. He looked downright spiffy. And I noticed he was not walking hunched over any longer, so it looked like there was no permanent damage from our little tussle.

He got into his fancy car, and I tailed him to another of the up-and-coming electronics plants out on the north end of town. Not far, I couldn't help noticing, from the parking lot where Henry had dished out my dose of pain a while back. A coincidence probably, but I wondered about it just the same.

He parked in the employees-only section of the lot and acted like he knew where he was going when he disappeared inside the place. The name on the front of the plant claimed it to be Haloran Computer Systems, Inc., a division of Haloran Industries. In very large letters.

I sat in my rent-a-heap with binoculars handy for quite some time, but I suspected that I was wasting my time and was right about it. Henry didn't see sunlight again until the lunch hour, and then he was with a gaggle of others dressed much the same as he was. They car-pooled it away to get a bite somewhere, and frankly I wasn't interested in going with them. It seemed pretty damn obvious that this was new employment for my boy and not just a job application. I pulled out to reclaim my Jeep, get a bite myself, and head over to G&G.

Cathy had to buzz Glen from beyond the guard on duty

114

at the research room, and he did not look like he appreci-
ated being disturbed, although he tried to act polite about
it.

"What's on your mind, Carl?"

"I wanted to show you something, Glen. Could you
come out to my Jeep for a minute?"

He frowned but said he would. As soon as we were
outside, I explained. "I didn't want to talk indoors, that's
all. I don't have anything in the Jeep."

"I see." He hesitated. "Frankly, Carl, I was not sure
you were still interested in my make-believe problems."

"Make-believe? You never heard that from me."

"I . . ." He started off with a lot of heat in his tone, but
that died almost as quickly as it had come. "You're right,
of course. I apologize."

"There's no reason to apologize, but you might tell me
what's wrong."

He shrugged. "I'm just nervous, I guess. None of my
people like the idea of having a guard lurking around the
place. I can't blame them, I suppose. And Junior has been
angry at me all morning over the same thing. He feels
affronted, although Lord knows he should understand more
than anyone else how important this project is to us." He
smiled. It was weak, but it was a start. "So I am perhaps
touchier than usual today. Now. What is on your mind,
Carl?"

"First, I am still very much interested in your problems,
Glen. I haven't been able to accomplish much of anything,
but I'm still trying. I want you to know that."

The smile came a little easier for him this time. "I know
that."

"Okay. Anyhow, a couple weeks ago when you first
told me what was going on, you said your drawings of one
component were ripped off by a competitor. I'm sure you
told me who that was, but I've forgotten."

"Well, I have not. Believe me."

"That wouldn't have been Haloran by any chance?" I
asked.

"Your memory is not as bad as you pretend, Carl. Yes,
it was Haloran." He made a face and muttered an impreca-
tion that was much stronger than his usual language.

"Tell me about them."

"If you wish, but it is a fairly standard background for the industry. A group of very bright and very ambitious young men got together with an idea and plunged into the world of the computer. They started with limited capital and unlimited ideas, subcontracted the construction of their initial components, and hit the market like a solid-brass bowling ball. They've been growing by leaps and bounds ever since."

"You said construction. They're in hardware, then?"

"Right. Exactly where I want to go with my Rainbow Drive, except now they are manufacturing entire systems."

"Would the Rainbow be valuable to them?"

Goodroe snorted. "To Haloran or to IBM or to anyone in between. Compatibility, Carl, that's the key to the Rainbow. It will extend the storage and therefore the usefulness of anyone's hardware equipment. Interchangeability with various hardware systems is the heart and soul of my design. Do you . . . think you have something?"

I shook my head. "Not really. I'd like to be able to tell you something definite, but I just can't. Not yet, but maybe it won't be long."

I really would have liked to be able to tell the man something, but what? My list of suspects was the exact same one he would already have been able to come up with on his own: everyone who worked for him and everyone he knew. Big deal. I was being an awfully big help to him.

Still, Henry Blair's new employment was a starting point. I would just have to see where it went from there.

We chatted for another moment or two, but Glen wanted to get back to his work behind that locked door.

Since I had nothing else better to do at the moment, I wandered back inside behind him and wasted the rest of the afternoon trying with no success whatsoever to beat Junior Goodroe at some of his beloved video games.

Galaxians was my favorite of the ones he had on hand since it is a straightforward game of shooting the attacking bad guys before they can shoot you. Frogger kind of intrigued me in a way, except that I am no damn good at it; my frogs always get squished on the pavement once the game speeds up.

And Junior's half-developed prototype of his own game, well, that mazelike contest was no contest at all as far as I was concerned. He was into traps and patterns and monsters popping up anywhere to blast the good guy—ships or robots, he hadn't quite decided yet—in the back. Not my style or something, but whatever the reason, I just couldn't fathom any of it and quickly went back to the simpler realms of Galaxians and Frogger and Pac-Man.

The kid was also no pleasure at all to be around. He had been too talkative to begin with. Now he was barely willing to snarl. Not just at me, but at everyone on the staff. He seemed to really have his nose out of joint lately, and I guessed he was still upset about the guards on the research room.

25

I wanted to get inside Haloran Computer Systems somehow, but the obvious solution of applying for a job there was out of the question. Aside from the fact that Henry Blair could and would recognize me anytime I let him get within a block of my binocular-draped neck, there was also the simple truth that I don't have a single skill that a computer manufacturer would consider remotely worthwhile.

I mean, breaking horses, throwing a rope, and having fast fun on a motorcycle are all well and good. But they don't exactly fit in with today's notions of modern technology.

As a matter of pure fact, it was something of a comeuppance for me to realize just how damned ill-prepared I would be if I ever—curse the thought—had to go out and *work* for a living.

It was enough to make a strong man shudder. So I did. Yuck.

Anyhow, with that out of the question, I had to content myself with some more long-distance observation. I found a hillside that some optimistic realtor was offering with industrial zoning not too far from the Haloran plant and isolated from the workaday traffic along Electronics Row. It was safe enough, in fact almost necessary considering the terrain, to use the Jeep up there, so I traded my binoculars for a spotting scope.

Henry, it seemed, was moving in a rarefied atmosphere these days. For the driver of a delivery van it was quite a step up in the world. His luncheon companion was usually a well-dressed older man. It really blew me away when I tracked him to his parking space that afternoon and, that night when the lot was empty, got close enough to read the reserved sign.

The guy was no less than the plant manager. John Trask by name. His was the only sign with the first name written out instead of indicated by initial only. I wondered if that was supposed to be considered a perk of rank somehow.

Regardless, I was damn well impressed that my former van driver was lunching with a plant manager these days. It seemed most curious strange, it did. A reward for good and valuable services? Possible. Entirely possible.

Still, if Henry was still up to any sort of skulduggery that would injure Glen Goodroe and G&G Electronics, he must have been doing it by telephone. He sure never went near G&G.

Henry's nighttime personal habits remained unchanged despite his apparent rise in social status.

It was still fast-food burgers and a stop at a nude bar for my pal Henry. The only major change was that he had switched his loyalties away from the Cat's Meow to a similar joint on the north side of town on the other end of Nevada Avenue. I couldn't decide if that was a matter of convenience, since the new joint was closer to his work, or if he did not want to risk going back to the same bar where I had found and had pounded him. Either way, he didn't go back to the Meow.

Good old Henry, though, had at least given me another name and face to watch. If Henry was, or had been, the go-between in Glen Goodroe's problems, John Trask was the most likely buyer of information.

26

"You don't look very busy."

Sandy shook her head. "I'm not." She was curled up in a comfy armchair with one of those recipe-filled women's magazines that they sell by the checkout counters in all grocery stores. She was wearing jeans and a shirt that looked like it might have been one of Junior's rejects, but she managed to look downright fetching in spite of that.

"Would you like to go for a walk?"

"I . . . don't know that that would be a good idea, Carl."

"Just a walk and a talk. I won't lay a glove on you, I promise. I . . . want to talk to you about something in private." That gambit just had to work. I've never yet met a pretty girl who couldn't out-curious any cat you'd care to name.

It worked. She wasn't smiling exactly but she did get her coat from the closet and join me for an evening stroll. Her father was hunched over some papers in the family room. Junior had gone off somewhere, which he did quite a lot, but he might return at any time.

Sandy set off at a very businesslike pace, and if I hadn't been in pretty good shape I might have had some trouble keeping up with her. She was heading uphill, toward an area of lots as yet unspoiled with houses, where the view of the distant city lights lying in the bowl below us was impressive. She wasn't breathing very heavily when finally she stopped. But then, neither was I. I got the impression that that was a disappointment to her.

"What was it you couldn't talk about with my father there, Carl?" She was looking at me like she expected the

120

answer to be a lewd one. It might have been, too, except that it was so apparent that she did not want to play.

"Relax, Sandy. I'm not intent on taking you places you don't want to go."

"I've heard that before, once or twice."

"Of course you have. Anyway, what I wanted to talk to you about was this business down at the plant that's worrying your dad. I could use your help with something, and I don't want to go to him with it. In fact, I don't want him to know anything about it."

"Why?" Very blunt, very suspicious. "He hasn't told me very much about whatever it is that is bothering him. I don't know that I could help."

"Look, the reason I don't want him to know anything about it is that the man has been on edge for better than a week now. He's worried. I don't want to make things worse by giving him any false hopes that I can help when I probably can't. I'm just . . . milling around right now. I'm not at all sure of what I'm doing, you see—"

"I don't see," she interrupted.

"That's reasonable. Neither do I. Anyhow, I only have the slimmest of slim chances to find out things I need to know if I'm going to be any help to your dad. Even after all this time, I'm still in the dark. Just floundering around from here to there and hoping something will start to make sense eventually. The point is, if your dad thinks I'm onto something, he will get to hoping about it, and the way these things usually turn out, well, I wouldn't want to be that cruel to such a nice man. Do you understand what I'm saying?"

"I don't know. I do know that I don't understand very much about you. I know that I don't really approve of the way you apparently live. You have no roots, Carl."

"That's an odd thing to hear. I'm living on land my great-grandfather homesteaded. There have been Hellers on it ever since."

"That isn't what I meant."

"Be that as it may, I'm still trying, in my own rootless, feckless, footloose way, to help a man I consider to be a superior human being. I *like* your father. I want to help him. I don't want to give him any false hopes. Can you understand that much?''

She nodded.

"All right, then. It doesn't have to be any more complicated than that.''

"What is it you want me to do?''

"First I want you to keep it to yourself and not tell your father. Or even Junior. He might just tell your dad if you tell him. Can you do that?''

She hesitated.

"It's no big deal,'' I said. "No cloak-and-dagger stuff. I just need an entrée to a place where I can't go by myself.''

"I don't understand.''

"You won't unless you can tell me you won't hurt your father by raising unfounded hopes.''

She thought for a moment more. "I can make you a conditional promise that I'll keep it to myself.''

"What's the condition?''

"If I decide that you are wrong and that he needs to know about it, I'll tell him.''

"That sounds fair enough. Actually we're both making a bigger deal out of this right now than it deserves. I just want to keep an eye on a particular person, you see, and he frequents a club where I'm not a member. Your father does belong, and I understand you have privileges there as part of the family. So what I want you to do, Sandy, is to let me take you to dinner a few times. Just sit there and enjoy the meal and a drink afterward. No big deal.''

"Who is the man?''

It was a perfectly logical question, and if I was guessing wrong about Sandy Goodroe, if she wasn't as innocent as I had come to believe, then I was giving myself away. Almost as bad, Glen Goodroe had been getting *really* uptight lately, and if she told him about my suspicions, he might make some direct accusations that would guarantee I'd never learn anything about John Trask and Haloran Computer Systems.

"He's a big cheese with one of your father's competitors. His name is Trask.''

She looked blank at the name. "Which competitor?''

"Haloran."

"That's the company that took out a patent on one of Daddy's ideas."

"Uh-huh."

"Do you think they are going to do the same with his new invention?"

"He's doing everything he can to prevent that."

"So I've heard. Junior really got mad at him about being locked out of the R-and-D room. So did half of the staff, the way I heard it. He got Junior calmed down, but I guess everyone else is still upset about all the sudden secrecy."

"Yeah, well, I want to find out if this Trask is having any contact with anyone from G&G, Sandy. He can't at the Haloran plant, of course. Any G&G people meeting him there would be a dead giveaway. But I understand a lot of people in the industry belong to this club where Trask goes most evenings. I know I've seen familiar faces going in the door, but I can't see what goes on inside because I'm not a member."

"What club is that?"

"It's called the After Byte. B-y-t-e, they spell it. I guess that's supposed to be English or something."

Sandy laughed. "You don't know much about computers, do you, Carl?"

"Not hardly."

" 'Byte' " is pronounced like 'bite.' It's a unit of memory in computereze. So the club's name is a play on words. After bite. After eating. It's a bottle club of sorts. Very relaxed and casual. A lot of the people in the business like to go there because of the common interests."

I smiled. "See? I knew you could help. Do you go there too?"

"Not really. I was there once or twice with Daddy and Junior, but everyone was talking shop. Computers aren't really my thing, even if I have been exposed to them for years and years. Certainly they aren't my idea of an evening's conversation."

"So no one there would be likely to recognize you as Glen Goodroe's daughter?"

"I wouldn't think so."

"That's perfect, Sandy. Would you get me in, then?"

She nodded. "I suppose so."

"Good. I don't know that it will help at all, but I want to find out."

"When do you want to go?"

"Just about every night," I told her, "at least for a little while. I can't really judge that until I see what it's like in there."

"One thing, Carl."

"Hmmm?"

"This isn't just some sort of artifice to . . . ?"

"To get you out alone? No. I wouldn't do that."

"Good, because . . . Up on the hill that time. I don't want a repeat of that performance. You should understand that, Carl. No passes or the deal is off."

"I understand." Up to a point I guess I did, too. Hands off; that I could understand. And of course she was entitled to her choice in the matter. What I couldn't understand was why she had been so receptive for those few seconds before she turned it all off and presented the cold shoulder.

Still, the choice was hers to make, and I had no right to argue with it. Regret it, sure, but not to argue.

"Not to worry," I told her.

27

Sandy took a small sip of her Smith and Curry and set it back down in front of her. She stared into the frothy white surface of the drink, not looking my way. She had been doing much the same thing for the past half-hour.

"You're awfully quiet tonight."

She shrugged but did not answer. I wanted to reach out and touch her, comfort her through whatever it was that was bothering her, but I was not sure how she would receive that and I did not want to make her any more uncomfortable than she obviously was already.

Damn she looked nice tonight. She was wearing a severely simple white dress that accented her figure and the flow of her hair. She looked heartbreakingly lovely. And very sad.

"I'm a pretty good listener," I ventured.

We were in the After Byte. Again. By now we were accepted by the staff as regulars at the small, dark table in the back corner. I wondered what the waiters thought about our constant attendance there. Probably thought we were lovers with roommates or spouses who kept us away from our homes, I decided. I almost wished they were right about it. That at least would have implied some future relief from the catch I felt in my throat whenever I looked at this girl.

"Is there anything—?"

"Please," she interrupted. Her voice was soft but it had an edge to it.

"Sorry." I took a drink of my Coors but the normally clean, crisp flavor of the brew was lost on me this time. It could have been club soda for all the pleasure I got out of it, and I am not one of those fancy-dans who gets anything from drinking carbonated water no matter what kind of label they put on the bottle or how much they charge for the stuff these days. I reached for a cigarette, toyed with the idea of cutting down on my smoking just long enough to heighten my anticipation of smoking, and then lit up.

"Carl."

"Mmm?"

"I'm sorry." She was still looking into her drink but apparently some slight improvement was in progress.

"It's all right."

"It isn't."

"We could argue about it. Maybe even get into a good fight. Would that make you feel any better?"

"No, it . . . isn't you I'm upset about."

"That makes me feel better anyway. I was beginning to wonder."

Sandy's shoulders rose and fell with a sigh that I could see but not hear.

"Do you want to talk about it?"

"No. I don't know. There isn't anything you can do anyway."

"Probably true, but like I said, I'm a good listener."

She sighed again. This time loud enough to reach me across the table. "Anyway, it happens all the time. They always get over it eventually." She looked up and met my eyes for the first time in quite a while. "Actually I suppose I should thank you. They've both been on their good behavior since you came."

"Which means you are talking about your dad and your brother, right?"

She nodded. She looked unhappy. "Junior and Daddy, well, they fight all the time. They were at it again today. I wish they could stop."

"It's natural enough, you know."

"That is what I keep telling myself, but I don't know. Junior resents everything Daddy does. And Daddy isn't much better. I don't think he lets you know, but he doesn't have much respect for Junior either. He teases him all the time about Junior's silly games. I can understand that, sort of, but it just makes things worse between them."

She paused and I waited for her to continue. She looked at me again. "Did you know that Daddy has a ladyfriend?"

"Your father is a very normal, perfectly healthy male human being, Sandy. It would only be remarkable if he didn't need that kind of contact."

"I know that. I know it intellectually anyway. It's a little harder to accept on the emotional level."

I nodded. I knew what she meant. One's parents are not supposed to be people, they are supposed to be parents. There is a difference.

"Junior doesn't even try to understand it on any level. He just adds it to his list of resentments. And Daddy, well, I suppose I shouldn't complain. I'm still Daddy's little girl and all that. But poor Junior can't do anything right. Daddy really wants him to be involved in the software part of the business and forget about those games. I think that makes Junior all the more determined to develop a game he can sell. I don't think the money would even make any difference to him, he just wants it to be a success so he can rub Daddy's nose in it and prove he was right."

"Is that what they were fighting about today?"

"Yes. Sort of. Junior was yelling at Daddy about not wanting him to be a success and trying to sabotage his game by keeping him out of the research room, and Daddy was yelling back about Junior being selfish and not thinking about the family's future and things like that. It got pretty nasty."

Which explained why Junior hadn't been at dinner with the family that night and why Glen had been so quiet at the table. I was just as happy I had missed all of that.

"They ended with Daddy taking some really low cuts at Junior and making a big, sarcastic show of leading him to the door and telling the guards they were to let his little boy—that's the way he put it, too, dammit—that they should let his little boy in anytime so he could play his games." Sandy shook her head. "If I'd been Junior I think I would have walked right out of there."

"What did he do?"

"He gave Daddy a look that I hope I never get from anybody, but he went into the research room and shut the door. I haven't seen him since, and I'm worried about that

too, Carl. Junior usually sulks in his room when he's
feeling offended, but this time he didn't come home. I'm
really worried about them this time."

I shook my head and took a drink of the beer. People!
Give us some troubles and we'll make the most of them.
Give us any easy go of it and we'll invent some troubles.

I wasn't particularly surprised that Glen and his son
were throwing off sparks when they grated on one another,
and I wasn't surprised either that they hadn't let me see
much of it during my visit. We all try to hide our private
sides from strangers in our homes.

Come to think of it, that might be an answer to a lot of
problems. Everyone should make it a point to keep a
houseguest around. Kind of like a pet. Of course we'd
have to make sure we rotated the guests frequently. If one
stayed around long enough to be accepted, the effect would
be destroyed. And they should always be strangers. A
trend like that, forcing good behavior on us in spite of
ourselves, could be real interesting. But then, I thought,
maybe it would just make our blowouts more extreme
when they finally did come. Maybe what I was advocating
there was not family harmony after all but a dramatic rise
in the incidence of assaults and wife-beatings. People!

"They'll get over it," I said reassuringly.

She gave me a wan smile. "I suppose. They always
have before."

"Where do you fit into it?" I was curious not so much
about where she actually did fit, which I thought I already
knew anyway, as about where she *thought* she fit. A
person's perceptions about him- or herself can be very
interesting things and do not necessarily match the facts of
any given situation. So I was really interested in her
answer.

"As far as Daddy is concerned," she said, "I'm still his
darling daughter. I can do no . . . What is it?"

For the first time in days I was suddenly oblivious of
this pretty girl who was in my company. I was staring
across the room toward John Trask's table.

28

Two very excited Haloran employees had come hurrying in to join the boss at his table, and one of those people was my old pal Henry Blair. I was grateful now for the low level of lighting in the club, although for night after night I had cussed it for not letting me see Sandy Goodroe better.

The second man was one I had seen entering and leaving the Haloran plant, although never before with Blair. He was dressed in a suit and tie, as would be expected for a visit to the club, but Henry was wearing blue jeans and a casual shirt. Not hardly the normal attire for a place like this. Both Henry and the other man looked animatedly pleased with themselves. They bent over and began whispering in Trask's ears. I beckoned Sandy to lean forward.

"I want you to turn around in a minute, real casual about it, and take a look at the two men at Trask's side, Sandy. One of them is the fellow who used to drive the Diplomat pickup van out at your father's place. I want you to tell me if you recognize the other one."

Sandy looked pleased, like she was glad all of this cloak-and-dagger nonsense was finally going to give us something to do besides soak up drinks we did not particularly want.

She did as I'd asked. When she turned back she said, "I know I've seen him before, but I don't remember his name. Is it important?"

"I don't know. He isn't one of your father's people anyway, right?"

"Oh no. I'd recognize him for sure if that were so."

"All right, then."

The men had finished with their conversation. They

stood and waited while Trask, grinning broadly, pulled a wallet from his inside coat pocket.

The fold of leather turned out to be a checkbook. He got a pen from another pocket, wrote out the check, and gave it to Henry Blair. I was wishing I was in a position to read the thing. Certainly this was a departure from the normal course of events for Trask, and Henry Blair's part in it made me doubly suspicious of what might be going on.

Trask certainly had not been expecting them and it was just as plain that he was mighty happy about whatever they were telling him.

He gave the two a thumbs-up sign and toasted them with his glass as they headed for the door.

"Do you have any money, Sandy?"

"Why?"

"Please, just answer the question."

"Yes, of course."

"Good. Call a cab and take yourself home, girl. I want to go see a man about a check."

She looked puzzled, but she didn't argue. I didn't hang around to make sure she could get home by herself.

I hurried outside, wishing I had thought to bring a topcoat, wishing I wasn't in the conspicuous Jeep that Henry Blair might recognize, wishing a lot of things but mostly hurrying. I didn't want to lose these two, whatever they were up to.

They were in Blair's car, which was a help. I knew it well enough already. And at night the glare of my headlights should be enough to keep Blair from noticing the Jeep in the city traffic.

They drove first to the Haloran plant, and I hung back and watched from a distance while the man I did not know got out of the passenger side of Blair's car and went inside. It seemed an odd hour to be opening the office. Blair pulled back into the scant flow of evening traffic on Garden of the Gods Road, and I tailed him from a safe distance.

He drove east to Nevada Avenue and turned south. The traffic was much heavier here, and I could stay with him with less danger of being spotted.

He took Nevada past the college to the downtown area,

jogged over to Tejon Street, and continued south past Acacia Park and the downtown banking district and the courthouse. There were few cars on the street here but all the street-side parking spaces were full. That has always amazed me. I've always wondered where all those people are going with the stores and the offices closed. None of my business, I suppose, but surely sloshing booze can't be all *that* popular in the few downtown bars.

Henry went a few blocks farther, to the miniature Combat Zone where the hookers and the adult booksellers plied their trades, and stopped in a parking slot across the street from the bar where the working girls hung out. I was seeing more of that place lately than I ever expected to, that was for sure. I hung a quick right and parked on the side street where Henry would be less likely to see my Jeep. I watched from the corner while Blair carefully checked to make sure his car doors were locked, then crossed the street into the well-remembered bar.

He had been in there before to pick up a girl for his weekend entertainment, but this was not a weekend night. And he was carrying John Trask's check in his pocket.

For a fleeting moment I wondered if it was something as simple as good old Henry doing a bit of helpful pandering for his boss.

But that hardly made any sense. Not that I thought Henry would be above that sort of thing, but I didn't think it would be Trask's style. Not with a street hooker anyway.

Besides, what self-respecting whore is going to risk accepting a check? Not bloody likely.

I found a pool of deep shadow at the entrance to a used-furniture store across the street from the bar and tried to make myself comfortable there. I wrapped the too-light fabric of my coat closer around my chest and once again berated myself for not bringing an overcoat.

I didn't have long to wait.

Henry's contact came out of the alley beside the bar in less than ten minutes. It didn't take any particular genius to recognize him.

He stopped at the back edge of the sidewalk and glanced hurriedly left and right, but all there was to see was a single pimp at the far end of the block having a talk with one of his girls. Both of them were bundled deep into furry coats against the cold; hers looked cheaply fake, while his was, even from a distance, quite obviously the real thing.

The contact satisfied himself that there was no one on the street that he should worry about, then hustled around the corner of the building and into the bar.

I felt sad when I watched him go in there. It was almost like a personal loss, although for whom I could not have said.

I sighed and hiked across the street to the damned bar. It was better, I figured, to break it up before things went any further than they already had.

The two of them were sitting at a table midway back in the narrow building. Henry Blair was facing my way but was not paying attention to the others in the place. He was in the process of passing over a check when I walked in on them.

I cleared my throat loudly enough to draw attention.

"We need to have a talk, Junior," I said.

29

It would have been all right, I think, but that damn scumbag bartender who hadn't been willing to fight me face-on thought he was pretty brave when the other guy's back was turned. He came at me from behind with a billy club of some sort.

I heard the scuff of his shoes on the floor, and by instinct—ain't no long-haired scientist going to tell me that humans don't have instincts—dropped as I turned.

Whatever it was he was swinging, the thing arced over my head fast enough to hiss through the air but my much-valued head was no longer in the place where he was aiming. Thank goodness.

The guy grunted with the force of his swing and grunted again when I brought a shoulder up into his paunch. The second grunt was considerably louder than the first had been.

His face turned white and I straightened up and popped him a couple hard, quick ones in the face. That brought the color back to his complexion faster than Revlon could have done the job.

He wasn't completely a coward, though. Or maybe at that point he was intent on defending himself now that the sneak attack had failed. Whatever, he raised the billy for a second assault on my skull.

I chopped him in the throat, and the man lost interest in further offensive activity.

By that time, though, Henry Blair and the pimps in the room had had time to figure out what was going on, and it seemed that they wanted a piece of me too. There were enough of them to make me question the wisdom of coming into the place, I'll tell you.

Blair was the first into action. He knocked Junior Goodroe out of his way and came around that table clawing and scrapping.

A looping right caught me over the ear hard enough to ring my bell, and he followed it with a left that did nothing to help my breathing.

Henry could be taken, though, and we both knew it.

I feinted a knee lift toward his crotch, and the memory of the last time we had squared off served me well. Henry flinched and dodged away, giving me time to get some air back into my lungs and bash him on the jaw with a clubbed fist that I swung backhand. The skin at the side of his mouth split, and from there things got kind of messy.

He went back to his punching, and for a few moments I was busy blocking and dodging.

Then some sonuvabitch who should have been minding his own business as a spectator planted a shot over my kidneys.

I didn't have any more time to fool around with Henry, so for the the second time I punted the ol' boy where it hurt the very worst.

I ducked low in time to take another blow from behind on the flat muscles of the back instead of in the kidneys. I spun to face the guy—turned out he was another of the pimps, but not one who had been in there the other day—and pummeled a quick combination into his belly.

The pimp was dressed mighty sharp, but the condition of his muscle tone didn't match the condition of his clothes. He turned an interesting shade of green and staggered off across the room.

There were two other pimps in the room, and both of them came flying in behind their partner.

For a little while there I was plumb busy. These two weren't much to look at, but they were willing. Between them they managed to put some sting on the sides of my face and head. What they'd done was confuse me. Both of them kept throwing flurries of punches, windmilling both arms until I didn't know which to block first or how to go about it, and as a result they were both of them scoring.

It finally occurred to me that I was playing at their way

as long as I kept trying to block everything all at once. That just can't be done.

So I picked one and concentrated on him, trying to will myself to ignore the other guy.

I blocked two punches, absorbed a bitch of a jolt on the forehead that split the skin there, and dropped Number One with a straight right to the heart and a clubbed fist to the neck. Not very pretty and definitely against the rules of formalized boxing, but it damn sure worked.

The remaining guy found himself alone, took a few more token jabs, and decided that this was the moment for some of that discretion that the old sayings tell about. He turned and ran out of the front door. The girls who had been sitting at the front tables had long since departed in that direction.

I turned back around thinking I'd better grab Junior and hustle him out of there before the cops arrived, but it was too late for that. I hadn't seen the kid go, but he was darn sure gone.

The little bastard hadn't even had the guts to stand and fight when he was caught.

I did some useless cussing and went over to where Henry Blair was curled up on the floor like a dying alley cat. I took a handful of shirtfront and yanked him halfway to his feet so I wouldn't have to bend over so far.

"Open the baby-blues, Henry, we have to have a talk."

He either didn't hear me over the screaming that was going on inside or he was ignoring me. It would have been difficult to tell which.

"Henry." I slapped him. He opened his eyes.

"The stuff Junior brought you, Henry. Where is it?"

This time I was pretty sure that he heard, but I got no better results.

"The drawings, Henry. I want them. Now." I held a balled fist under his nose, but that didn't work either. Either he was already in so much pain that he figured a little more couldn't hurt any worse or he was in such bad shape that he couldn't do anything about it.

I muttered a few strong oaths and dropped him.

The bartender had revived enough to begin crawling for the well behind the bar—or maybe for a weapon back there—and the offended pimps were sitting up and beginning to move around too. The girls and the last pimp had been gone long enough by now to call for reinforcements. I figured it was past time for me to think about making an exit.

"Henry!"

No response. Nothing. The poor bastard would be awfully glad when I went back up into my mountains, I figured.

Still, I couldn't leave Glen Goodroe's drawings for the Haloran people to admire.

I patted Blair's jeans down and came up with nothing but the usual wallet and keys and change. His shirt pockets were empty too.

Something was missing, and it was hanging on the back of the chair Henry had been using, miraculously still upright after all the commotion. I checked his coat pockets.

Eureka. A roll of 35mm film. Not exactly the tiny Minox cartridges that all the old spy movies require, but quite good enough. I appropriated the film, patted the coat pockets one more time—it would have been embarrassing to rip off a roll of dirty pictures and leave Glen's valuable drawings behind—and got the hell out of there. I'd had about all the excitement I wanted for one evening's entertainment.

30

Sitting in that family room was like being in a hospital room visiting a terminally ill friend. There was no way to offer comfort or good cheer.

Glen was huddled in his easy chair with his face gray and drawn. Sandy was sitting on the arm of the chair with her arms protectively curled around her father's shoulders. The discussion that had just taken place had been a bitch to get through.

"Is there no possibility that you could be wrong, Carl?" He didn't sound like he believed that. There was not even any trace of hope in his tone of voice. I suspect it was something he felt compelled to ask anyway.

"You can develop the film and know for sure," I suggested. "But I wouldn't hold out much hope, Glen. It's a very low-speed, fine-grained black-and-white Ilford. Not the sort of stuff you buy to take pictures of your girlfriend with. I think you'd have to go to a photo-supply store to get it, too. But you'll have to have it developed to know for sure."

I tossed the little metal caninster to him. He made no attempt to catch it. It landed in his lap and lay there with all three of us staring at it.

After a moment Glen reached down and picked it up. His sigh sounded like the weight of the entire world's sins was on his shoulders.

"No," he said slowly. "I think I should not trust having those drawings in a photo lab." He took the inch or so of leader that was protruding from the slot in the canister and pulled. It was a thirty-six-exposure roll and there was a lot of film in that small can. He exposed it to the lamplight with slow thoroughness and then let the

curling mass of undeveloped film fall to the floor beside
his chair.

"I am truly sorry, Glen," I said. It was so, so true but it
sounded terribly lame just the same.

"We know that," Sandy said when her father failed to
respond.

"Where has he gone? Where *could* he go?" Goodroe
asked of neither of us. He sounded numb, toneless.

"He had Trask's check in his pocket when he took off. I
don't know how much it was for, but . . ."

Glen was in shock but he was still capable of logical
thought. "That check will be stopped five seconds after
the bank opens tomorrow morning. A man who would
steal from a competitor is hardly the type to reward failure."

I hadn't thought of that, but Glen was probably right.
Largess in return for the good old college try gone awry
was hardly part of the corporate scene these days. Wherever he was, Junior was on his own now.

"I wonder . . ." Glen stopped and shook his head. I
could guess at some of the things he must have been
thinking and it was probably better that they were not said.

"This must be an awful night for him to have to go
through now," he said after a time. Under the circumstances it was an amazingly compassionate thing for the
poor bastard to be saying. Personally I would have been
beating my chest and wanting to beat on Junior. Certainly
some self-pity would have been forgiveable, but Goodroe
wasn't indulging. Instead he was worried about the welfare
of the sorry ingrate that he had raised.

I couldn't understand that. So perhaps it is just as well
that I've never become a father. I did not think I would be
up to the job at a time like this.

"I wonder if we might hear from him sometime." He
sounded like he actually hoped they would. I couldn't
understand that either, but then, I am not a very forgiving
person. I almost envied Glen Goodroe that ability.

"Of course we will, Daddy. Not right away, of course.
But sometime. I'm sure of it." Small comfort if any, but I
couldn't have thought of anything better. She patted her
father's shoulders and smoothed his hair back in a distinctly maternal gesture. I might not be much qualified for

parenthood but I thought that Sandy Goodroe had the stuff that tough, miserable job would require.

"Out there in the night somewhere . . . alone . . ." Glen shook his head. He was still thinking about the kid.

"If you want to find him," I said, "the police . . ." I shut up. Both of them were looking at me with a certain horror in their eyes.

Blowing the whistle on the kid, apparently, was unthinkable.

It was their decision to make, of course, and I guess I could understand it. Junior was too old to be chased as a runaway. It would take a criminal charge to get the cops interested in him. And that they were not willing to do.

I did some sighing of my own to go along with the ones the two of them were putting out.

"If you don't mind . . ." There was no point in trying to get their attention now. They weren't either one of them aware that I was anywhere around. I went off to bed, feeling about as low as I could remember being.

31

Glen didn't go to work the next morning. He was sitting slumped and miserable in his favorite chair in the family room again. Or still. I wasn't really sure which. He might have spent the night there.

"He will be all right, Carl. Truly he will," Sandy assured me. "He is a strong man, and he can survive this." She forced a smile that wasn't particularly convincing. I wondered if she was trying to convince me. Or herself.

While her father reacted to his misery by withdrawing, Sandy was reacting with activity. She prepared a breakfast large enough to serve the corps of cadets at the Air Force Academy, then was unable to stay still long enough to eat any of it. Her father wasn't interested either, and I had to force myself to get any of it down. The atmosphere in the Goodroe household was not what you would call conducive to a long, leisurely meal.

"I think, if you don't need me for anything . . ." I said just as soon as I thought I politely could.

"Of course. I understand."

I had caused about enough pain for these people, I figured. It was time I headed back up the pass to some simple pursuits like training horses and tending cattle. All the crap a city forces on the human condition was getting to me. "If there's anything I can do . . ." I let it hang there, wishing there might be something but knowing there was no comfort I had to offer to them. She shook her head.

I packed—it took only a few minutes—and loaded my gear into the CJ. I said my good-byes to Glen and was not even sure he heard them. It didn't matter.

At the door Sandy offered her hand for me to shake.

That one kiss was not going to be repeated even to say so long. But then, she did have other things on her mind at the moment. I shook hands with her.

"Are you sure there's nothing I can do?"

She shook her head, but her eyes cut away from mine. There was something, but she didn't want to ask it.

"What is it?" I insisted.

"Nothing. I can handle things here."

"I know that. So what is it?"

"I don't want to make you go out of your way."

"I wouldn't make the offer if I didn't mean it."

"It's nothing, really."

"So it's a tiny, insignificant nothing. Fine. What is it?"

"It's just . . . my horses. I haven't been out there in days. Yesterday I should have gone, but I got busy, and today . . ."

"And today you need to stay beside your father. He needs to have you near. Look, it's just a couple miles to the pasture. I'll stop there and check the water tank and make sure they're all right, then I'll head on up the pass. Okay?"

She responded with a very small smile but with a nod of her pretty head too. "Thank you."

I shook my head. "I don't know that you should thank me for anything, Sandy. I'm not sure your dad wouldn't rather lose the Rainbow Drive than find out what I had to tell him last night. I'm really sorry about that."

"I know." She looked thoughtful. "He would much prefer to lose the Rainbow than Junior. You know, if Junior had known that, none of this would have happened."

She was right about that, too. I was sure of it.

In spite of my best intentions, I bent down to brush her cheek with a brief kiss. I turned and practically ran to the privacy of my own Jeep and my own life. I really was not needed anywhere in their lives now.

I drove north instead of heading down toward U.S. 24 and fumbled in the console for a tape to raise my spirits. There is one I carry for special occasions when I don't want to get involved in the lyrics of the country music I love. That special tape always stays underneath the rest, though, so it won't be spotted by casual visitors. I plugged

it into the deck and surrounded myself with Rimsky-
Korsakov's *Scheherazade*. That piece is larger than any
troubles I might have, and it nearly always works when
I'm moping. It did this time too.

The pasture was only a few minutes away. I opened the
gate and pulled through, then went back to close it before I
drove on up to the stock tank. Sure the horses would
probably come to the Jeep to see if I had a handout for
them, but they weren't my animals and I wasn't about to
take any chances on letting someone else's stock out onto
a public highway.

I turned the volume up to three-quarter gain, enough to
make the side curtains flutter, and bounced across the
rough ground toward the slight hilltop where the well had
been drilled.

Damn!

I jammed the brakes on and came to a jolting stop that
killed the engine. The music sounded even louder with no
competition.

Not that I was paying any attention to what I was
hearing.

Past the stock tank and the foundation stakes for the new
plant, I could see the roof of a car parked just beyond the
hill. I was almost certain the car was Junior Goodroe's
sporty Datsun.

I restarted the CJ and began rolling uphill again. But
more slowly this time. Much more cautiously. I would
have been willing to put my money on the idea of the kid
being hundreds of miles away by now. Instead he, or at
least his car, was right there. I wondered what the hell he
was up to.

I wondered that right up to the point when the first slug
came sizzling down the hillside to plow an ugly gouge into
the sheet metal of my hood.

The second bullet blew my right-front tire as I was
trying to pull the Jeep around in a screamer of a turn. The
CJ lurched sideways, and the deflated tire and nearly bare
rim slid into one of those furrows any sensible man will
dig in his hillsides to capture runoff.

A little thing like that is not particularly serious when
you're driving a four-wheeler, of course. I could drive right

out of it, no sweat. All I had to do was get out and lock the hubs, then put it into four-wheel drive. Sure. Bend down and lock that exposed hub with a round-the-bend juvenile delinquent taking shots at me.

Damn him, I thought, but it was a little too late for that to do any kind of good.

He fired again, and the bullet passed through the soft top of the Jeep. It made an oddly hollow sound, like an untuned drum being hit with a mallet.

Time to leave, I decided. Very astute of me. I left the Jeep with speed if not grace.

32

Some people never learn. I am one of them. Junior—at least I couldn't think of anybody else who might be up there—was behind a pile of loose dirt at the top of the hill throwing bullets my way—from a handgun of some sort, thank goodness, and therefore with limited accuracy—and my own Smith & Wesson defensive system was miles away in a drawer in my bedroom. That was a bitch of a place for the thing to be when I needed it. Which I have warned myself about countless times. Sometimes I don't pay any more attention to my own advice, though, than to anyone else's. Now I was going to have to pay for it.

On the other hand, I really had no great desire to hurt Glen Goodroe further by blowing his son and heir away. The kid's neck I would cheerfully wring, but I didn't really want to kill him, and the guy who will tell you he can shoot to wound rather than kill is a first-class asshole or a liar or both. So maybe it is just as well that I wasn't armed. I don't know that my self-control would have extended to allowing Junior to shoot at me without me shooting back.

Still, the kid was under no tender illusions about the preservation of my as-yet-unpunctured flesh. He shot several times more, and the slugs whined off the hard-earth lip of the depression I was lying in. It was the same water-control cut my Jeep had dropped into when the tire went flat.

I found it a great pity that the furrow was deep enough to capture my CJ but a great relief that it was deep enough to contain my butt without anything protruding. You get some and you give some, I guess.

Another bullet ricocheted off the dirt, and I bellied a few yards farther along the ditch.

Several minutes went by in silence. I was undecided about how much of an improvement that was supposed to be. It was nice to know that he wasn't shooting at me for the time being. On the other hand, it made me wonder where he was and what the hell he was up to now that he was not up there firing. I poked my head above ground level and ducked back under cover immediately.

Nothing. I was more than half-expecting to draw his fire again, but there was no response.

I tried it again and stayed up a second or two longer this time. Still no response.

The third time I propped myself up on my elbows and left myself visible from the eyeballs upward. It was not really all that much of a risk. The place I had last seen him was at least seventy-five yards away, and there is nothing but sheer luck that will put a bullet from a handgun into a postcard-sized target at that range. Neither Junior nor I would ever be good enough to do it deliberately.

He was still there, all right. In fact he was perched on top of the dirt mound now. He saw me and waved. I waved back at him. Somehow I do not think your average combat infantry instructor would approve of that, but I did it without thinking.

"Out of ammunition, Junior?" I called.

"Sort of." The breeze was blowing off the mountains, down past him toward where I was lying. I could hear him quite clearly.

"Do you want to talk about it?"

He didn't say anything, but I could see him shake his head.

"I want to talk to you, Junior. About your father. He hasn't turned you in, you know. I haven't either, but I'm fixing to. Unless we talk this over first."

He sat there for a moment. "Come on up," he called.

"I can't say that I really trust you a helluva lot, Junior. Where's your gun?"

He reached to his waistband and pulled it out to where I could see. It was a smallish revolver, probably in one of the smaller calibers too. He held it pointed toward the sky and pulled the trigger. "No bullets," he called. He tossed the empty gun aside.

I would have to say that I felt considerably better after he did that. I stood up in plain sight.

"You wouldn't have another of those things handy, would you, Junior?"

"Nope. Just that one. Poppa gave it to me on my sixteenth birthday." I wonder if that was supposed to be significant somehow. And whether it was significant that the had called Glen Poppa. I couldn't remember him doing that before. Regression to a previous name for his dad and emotional age for Junior? It was worth wondering about.

"I'm coming up now. We can talk."

"Okay."

I took a step forward. And another. I felt rather naked once I was that far away from the protection of my hidey-hole. I could still make a dive for it now, but a few more steps and that would not be possible. I took a few more steps.

I stopped. The range was still long, but the kid was not especially cool and patient and rational or he would not be doing any of this. If he had a hideout gun on him, I figured, now would be the time for him to pull it.

He reached into his jacket, and I tightened all over. I was ready to spin and make a jump for that runoff ditch.

He pulled his hand out but there was no gun in it. Maybe he hadn't been lying after all. I took a few more steps up the gentle slope of the hillside.

It was still pretty far away, but believe me my curiosity about the thing was intense enough to make me look at it pretty hard. He was holding something small and rectangular in his hands. It looked like it might be an electronic control of some sort. Like one of those hand-held versions of the video games he was so damned fond of.

This kid was never far from one of his stupid games, I thought. I took another step or two up the hill. Junior watched me. He was smiling at me.

Something in that smile made me stop.

It's a damn good thing that I did.

A few yards in front of where I stood, the earth erupted

with a roar. There was a tremendous clap of noise and a gout of flying clods.

Concussion from the blast knocked me on my butt, and my ears had a dull, dead ringing in them.

Land mine? Where the hell would he have gotten hold of a land mine? Besides, if it had been any sort of shrapnel device, I would have been dead now. As it was I was feeling the effects of the blast and had been spattered with some dirt, but no serious damage had been done.

I bounced back up onto my feet and shouted some really choice cusswords at him.

I am absolutely, positively certain that I shouted at him. But I had to prove that by intent and past experience. I couldn't hear any of it. *I couldn't even hear my own damned voice.*

Did that scare me? You damn well better believe it did. It is one weird experience to know you are making noises but not be able to hear them.

I became suddenly, irrationally, but terribly afraid that Junior Goodroe was sneaking up behind me and I couldn't hear him coming.

I whirled around so fast I tripped myself. He wasn't there. I whirled again to face in another direction. Finally I got some small degree of control over myself and looked up the hill again. Junior was still perched on his mound of dirt with the little control box in his hands.

He was saying something, but I couldn't tell what it was. He was grinning. Pointing to the little box. Waving to me again.

The little prick had obviously touched off the explosion with his magic box. Glen Goodroe or no Glen Goodroe, if I'd had a gun now I would have shot him without hesitation. The little creep had tried to kill me.

Or had he? He was still grinning and pointing proudly at that box. I wondered if he was telling me that he could have taken me out with that first blast but hadn't bothered to. Yet.

He smiled and pointed off to my right. I looked where he was pointing. A second later there was another eruption of earth. Mount St. Helens out of a molehill. From a distance it was quite as spectacular as Old Faithful but a whole lot more lethal. Worst of all, I could feel the concussive shock wave reach me, but I couldn't hear the blast.

I looked back at Junior. He was saying something, and from the look on his face I could guess that it was a taunt. A come-and-get-me sort of thing.

Damn him anyway. Didn't he know that all I had to do was sit here and wait? Eventually someone would get around to calling the cops. They'd come. Surround his private little minefield. And about the time he blew one of them up, they would blow him away.

Damn all nice people anyway. If Junior Goodroe wanted to get his buns blown to bloody red scraps, what business was it of mine? Why should I care if Glen Sr. spent the rest of his days grieving for a son who wasn't worth a single one of the father's tears.

The hell with all of them. What I should do is go back to my Jeep to sit and wait for the cops to arrive.

That was exactly what I figured I should do.

I took another step up the hillside toward Junior.

33

How many of these damn things did he have?

One went up practically in my face. I ran to the right, and he met me with another. It was close enough to knock me flying. I rolled and tried an end run around the left, and yet another spray of silent earth rose up in front of me.

That one sent a clod of hard dirt into my chest. It hurt like hell, down deep in the muscle. I was lucky it hadn't been rock, though, or I likely would have been killed instead of just stunned.

I ended up sitting on the ground, stone deaf and by now spitting mad.

However he had laid these things out, and whatever he had used to make them, they seemed to be everywhere.

There was no worry now about exposing myself to gunfire, though, and I had what seemed like a decent idea if not exactly a brainstorm. I went back down to my CJ and locked the hubs so it could pull out of the ditch. Flat tire or no, it would still get a job of work done.

Up above, Junior was shouting something. I didn't know what he was saying but I hoped he was mad. Some pumping up of his blood pressure would give me some satisfaction even if it didn't do much to him.

The engine caught. It was strange. I couldn't hear either the starter motor or the engine but had to rely on the gauges and on a hint of vibration in the steering wheel to tell me it was running. It was awkward, but the deaf have to put up with that inconvenience every day. I . .·.

I stopped where I was and sat there in horror at the thought I had just had. I'd been assuming since that first blast that I was just stunned, that eventually, in an hour or a day or maybe even a week, my hearing would be just

149

fine again. That it would come back and all would be as it had been.

Now . . . I had no guarantee about that.

Thinking about the deaf, I might very well be thinking about myself. Now and for the rest of my life.

I slammed the transfer case into low range, put the transmission into low gear, and powered across the runoff ditch toward the miserable little sonuvabitch Junior Goodroe.

I was seeing red, and if I'd had my hands on the kid's neck at that moment he would not have lasted long.

The Jeep lurched and bounced on its three good wheels, bucking over the uneven terrain. I got up a few miles per hour and snapped the shift lever into second.

Junior picked that moment to hit another button for his hidden charges.

The front end of the Jeep was thrown into the air harder than any bucking bronc I ever sat. It was like doing a backflip off the high board.

The CJ turned turtle and ended up spinning slowly on the roll bar. I could feel the hard, lumpy ground rubbing my shoulders through the vinyl material of the top, and I was awfully glad that some bright soul had invented the roll bar for modern rec vehicles.

I still couldn't hear a thing. Hadn't heard any of the explosion or whatever grinding of metal might have followed it. But there was nothing wrong with my sense of smell.

Right now I could smell dry earth and the sharp, ugly scent of gasoline.

I got my bearings in the unfamiliar surroundings of an upside-down CJ, cut the ignition switch, and clawed my way out through what was left of the nearest door.

Junior was still where I had last seen him. He seemed to be getting quite a kick out of the whole thing.

My chest still ached, my ears were still ringing, and now my whole left side felt like a herd of mules had spent their day trying to stomp me into the ground. Come to think of it, I wasn't doing too damn well against this ninety-eight-pound weakling of a games player.

Damn you, I shouted beyond the silence that filled my

head. He didn't react so I didn't even know if any sound had gotten out that time.

I stood there and popped my jaw in a futile attempt to clear my ears, but this was a whole lot different from a simple change of elevation. I shook my head some, but that didn't do any good either.

Throughout it all Junior sat there calmly watching me, about as unreachable as if he had been at the top of Pikes Peak.

I didn't want to look at him anymore, so I looked at my Jeep. It was a bit of a mess. The forward running gear was twisted, and a good many parts were simply not there any longer. Radiator fluid and gasoline and who knows what else were forming puddles downslope from where it had come to rest. This was not my year to hang on to cherished motor vehicles. First the Beemer totaled and now the CJ. Pretty soon I would be down to a horse and saddle for everyday transportation. I looked back up the slope toward Junior and expressed myself on that subject. He seemed unimpressed.

Also unreachable.

I took another step toward him, and a spray of dirt flew up a few yards distant. Obviously a warning again.

That really made me mad. The little bastard was *playing* with me. Like this was another of his damned games. He . . .

I stopped and stared at him. He *was* playing a game. A potentially deadly game but a game nonetheless.

And this minefield of his. He hadn't dashed out here the night before and thrown the thing together. No way. Anything that complex would have taken a great deal of time to put together. Particularly since the charges were so very well camouflaged. I couldn't see the damn things even when I was standing practically on top of one of them. He hadn't done that overnight.

All right, dammit.

I quit reacting, quit running on the basis of anger and instinct, and tried to do some thinking as a change of pace.

The fools-rush-in approach had not gotten me very far. Maybe a new tack was in order here.

I stood straddling the gouged-out hole where a charge had already blown—there couldn't have been another there or the first detonation would have set them both off—and tried to get a closer look at Junior and his handy little do-it-yourself destruction box.

The control mechanism was not very big. I had mistaken it for a hand-held game when he first brought it out. Yet he was using it to set off charges over here and then over there and then somewhere else again. It stood to reason that he would not have a separate button on a little thing like that box for each charge he had laid. Therefore he had to key the commands somehow to determine which charge would be blown by the firing button, or switch, or whatever it was. I was much too far away to see any of the details on the thing.

Anyway, that meant he had to manipulate it somehow, and that would take a certain amount of time.

I thought about those games Junior was so terribly fond of. Virtually all of them used reaction time as part of the problem the player had to overcome when the monsters or the robots or the space torpedoes came swarming in on him.

To Junior that kind of manipulation would be part of the game.

To me, that might mean that if I could swarm him, move inside his minefield or move through it faster than he could key his detonations, then I could defeat him.

What it came down to, I guess, is that Junior Goodroe was the player at the video controls. And I was the alien spaceship trying to reach his home base.

The difference was that here the alien would bleed real blood if one of those charges went off under his feet. The alien could die a real death.

Speed, though. Speed might give me the edge I needed to get to him.

If I could rush past his warning charge and get up that hill faster than Junior could key his successive mines, I just might have a chance to reach him.

I began walking upslope again. I braced myself for the explosion, anticipating it, and of course I did not have to worry about flinching at the sound. There would be no sound anyway.

The earth erupted four yards in front of me, and I could feel the hot air of the explosion push at me, but not hard enough to do any damage.

As soon as I saw the geyser of dirt, I ran forward. Or tried to. The deep bruising in my side wasn't so bad at a walking pace, but at a run it was unbearable. I was hobbling more than running, galumphing along on one strong leg and a weak one, and I knew before I had gone three paces that it was not nearly fast enough.

Another sheet of earth flew up just ahead of me, and I stopped.

Junior was up there laughing at me and motioning for me to come ahead, damn his eyes. It probably was just as well that I couldn't hear his taunts. I really didn't need to. I was mad enough without that.

I turned and began limping back down the slight slope. I was back to the Jeep before it occurred to me that that last explosion had not flown straight up into the air the way the others had done. This one, a little higher up the slope and closer to Junior's "base," had spread out into a sheet of dirt, whereas the others had been geyserlike upward blasts.

A poorly laid charge? I wondered. Or a complexity in the defenses?

The key to Junior, I reminded myself, was in his bloody video games. And so many of them, most if not all, were layered in increasing degrees of difficulty. Junior's own game . . .

Why hadn't I thought of that before now? He had told me so much about that game of his. I had paid so very little attention to any of what he had said.

I did distinctly remember him telling me, though, that his game became increasingly complex as the player advanced.

So that sheetlike charge was no accident. There would be a whole hillside layer of those spreading charges to get through.

And beyond that? I was willing to believe almost anything. Rocks shaped over the charges to form a civilian version of shrapnel? It would be logical.

Speed was still the only weapon I could think of to use against him.

The way I was feeling now, hurting up and down most of my abused body, speed was something I was not going to be able to provide for myself. I looked at the wrecked Jeep. I wasn't going to find it there either.

Dammit. I found myself looking off toward the highway. I wasn't at all sure of whether I wanted the cops to come kill this kid or not.

34

I limped down the slope toward the gate. My idea was that if Junior really wanted me—which was still in question, since it might be just another game as far as he was concerned—I would quit going after him. If he really wanted me, he could damn well leave his toy behind and come after me. I had no doubt at all that I could cope with him once I got him out from behind his wall of land mines.

I went partway down and turned to look back up toward him. I couldn't hear anything, and at this distance I couldn't see if his mouth was moving, so I had no idea what kind of reaction I was getting from him. If any.

For sure, though, he did not put aside his magic box and come chasing down after me. He continued to sit there on his dirt pile.

King of the Mountain? I thought. Is that the game now? Modern electronics and modern explosives melded with video-gamesmanship to play the ages-old game of childhood? I could believe that of him. He must really have wigged out after I burst his little bubble.

But no, I was not really responsible for this. Not with all the work that must have gone into this before I ever arrived on the scene. The kid had been weird to begin with. Last night had just put a match to a fuse that was already in place. I shook my head.

Something touched me on the back of the neck, and I jumped half a foot off the ground. I think I might have screamed too.

It was hot and wet and it was after me, and . . .

And it tickled. Tickled?

155

The cold chills I was feeling subsided, and I began to laugh at myself.

Sure enough, when I turned around there were Sandy Goodroe's pet horses. It was the bay that was nuzzling me. The sorrel was a couple steps behind. I spoke to them, or tried to, and scratched the bay's poll.

I had forgotten about the horses after getting that look at Junior's Datsun. The poor things must have been in a panic with all that blasting going on. Or then again, maybe it hadn't bothered them. Horses can be awfully notional that way. A fair number of them will stand firm in the face of gunfire. Yet that same fool animal might be utterly terrorized by a gum wrapper blowing through the grass.

Of these two the bay seemed quite content with some human companionship, while the sorrel was breathing heavily and showed some sweat between his forelegs. I guessed that he had been upset, while the bay remained calm during the recent fireworks.

"Calmer than I was I'll bet," I told the bay from the ringing silence in my head. The deafness was annoying, and I popped my jaw some more and rubbed at my own ears as well as the bay's.

"You aren't worried about a thing, are you, boy? Of course not. The grass will be here tomorrow no matter what us stupid humans do to each other, and . . ."

I stopped. Very, very faintly I thought—it might have been imagination or wishful thinking—but I sure thought I could kind of hear a little bit of that.

"Testing one, two, three," I announced to the uninterested horse. "Testing."

A little. Just a little, maybe. It was enough to give me some hope that I was not permanently deaf, and that was quite a lot. I began to smile. Couldn't help it. I wanted to shout. I shouted. I could almost hear it this time.

I grinned at the bay horse and rubbed him under the jaw. "Looks like you did that much, old boy. Now, if you could just tell me how to get through ol' Junior's line of defenses up there . . . Sonuvabitch! I guess you told me that too."

Speed. That was the ticket. Speed was something I

didn't have with my leg and side deeply bruised and my chest still shooting pains.

But this four-legged beastie had more speed than any human will ever claim. A Quarter Horse, any Quarter Horse, is bred for sprints. Powerful outbursts of raw speed over short distances.

If anything could move through Junior's ring faster than Junior could key his destructive little box, this horse should be it.

Of course the animal might panic in the face of those geysers. It could throw me off plumb onto the next charge. It could be killed itself.

Hell, lots of things *might* happen. The question was, did I want to make another try to take that kid or did I want to wait until the cops arrived so they could take him? The logical, obvious, and probably wise thing to do would be to wait and let someone else worry about it. They could do the job, and if Junior Goodroe got killed in the process, it was his tough luck.

And Glen's. And Sandy Goodroe's.

I had rather scant concern for G. Goodroe Junior at the moment, but those others were mighty nice people. They deserved better.

Besides, I was mad enough that I just plain wanted him myself.

"Hold still, knucklehead," I told the bay.

The horse was wearing his halter, and while I despise the dangerous habit of turning a horse loose in pasture with a halter in place—they can hang up on posts or limbs or what-have-you and strangle the animal—this time I was glad about it.

I'd never ridden the animal and had no idea how well it might respond to knee pressure and weight shift, so I figured I needed a makeshift bridle to make sure I could point him where I wanted him. My belt would do for that. I slipped the belt through the halter ring under his jaw. There was not enough of it to give him a pair of reins, but it would serve as an Indian-style single rein. Held on one side of the head, you had a neck rein in the one direction and a direct rein in the other. Unfancy but useful.

"Hold still, stupid." I took a handful of mane and

swung onto him. The bay stood rock-steady. I wished I
could remember if this one was the English-trained horse
or the games horse, but I couldn't. One would jump better
and the other would pivot and turn better. I hoped it didn't
make a difference once we started after Junior.

I bumped the horse forward up the slope. Junior was
still up there on his dirt pile. I wondered if he realized
what was coming. It would be too much to expect, but
there was also the hope that he would be sensitive about
the idea of killing horses, or at least his own sister's
beloved pet, and might let me ride right on in.

Nope. Too much to ask. A spray of dirt lifted into the
air about fifteen yards in front of the bay. The horse shook
his head but otherwise ignored it.

The sorrel, behind us, had been following close on the
bay's tail, but now it wheeled and went into a bucking run
back toward the safety of the gate and the roadside. It
wanted no part of all this noise.

Noise. There had been some of that too. I hadn't heard
the explosion very loudly, but at least I had heard it blow.

I pulled the bay to a stop and waved to Junior. He
waved back.

"That answers that," I told the horse. "Your buddy up
there isn't going to wait for us to ride up on him. The next
question is, which way do we want to go up?"

There were a couple possibilities there, and either one
was sheer guesswork. Junior could well have prepared for
a simple frontal assault—most of his cherished video games
played in a single direction—or he might have ringed the
entire foundation site with his pattern of mines. I'd have
given a bunch to know which. If he was prepared in only
one or two directions, the smooth move was to go around.
But if he was running it in a full circle, the best bet would
be to go over the area where he had already expended
some of his firepower.

But which?

"Let's take a tour of inspection, yo-yo," I told the
horse.

I rode around to my right. Junior made no attempt to
stop me. He stayed where he was and swiveled slowly to
face me as I rode. The magic box was in his hands, but he

was not fingering it that I could tell. That would have been
a dandy clue to his layout if he had been nice enough to
key in his minefield ready for explosion until I reached a
bare patch. No go, though. He just sat there watching. I
popped my ears again. I thought I could hear the footfalls
of the horse, but that might have been wishful thinking.

The back part of the Goodroe property was choppier and
steeper. There was a gentle rise from the road along the
front, but in back there was much more of a grade. I rode
around below Junior's Datsun.

"You know, horse," I muttered, "if that knothead's
view is blocked a little bit, that wouldn't be a bad thing for
us."

I still didn't know if Junior had any defenses back here.
If so, none of them had been used yet. I rubbed the back
of my neck and shot my jaw again. My hearing was
definitely coming back now.

"Come on down, Junior. You've played long enough,"
I shouted. It didn't do any good. He said something, but
my hearing was not good enough yet for me to understand
what he said. Whatever it was, he sat right where he was.

"You ready, horse?" I couldn't hear any answer from
him either.

I took a big handful of mane, made sure I had a firm
seat just behind the bay's withers, and thought fleetingly
about John Wayne. Somehow this wasn't quite the same as
his charge against Ned What's-his-name in *True Grit*, and
I felt no desire to hold the end of my belt between my
teeth. I took a deep breath.

The bay surged ahead when I gouged him with my
heels. I gave in to an impulse and let out with my own
version of a rebel yell. "Eeeeee-yahhhhhhhh!"

35

The bay's right shoulder dropped, and I damn near pitched off him.

Damn, I thought. A stumbler I didn't need right now.

I yanked him hard to the right to get myself seated back over him again, and a gout of earth rose just to the left.

Junior wasn't scaring me now. He was trying to set them off directly under the horse's belly. I jinked back to the left.

The explosion this time was to the rear. Speed. It was helping. Junior was going to have to break the pattern to key his box now.

I headed the bay straight up the hill toward him for several stretching strides, then darted the animal left and back to the right.

A spray of clods swept the hillside ahead and to the left. You pushed the wrong one, you little bastard, I told Junior wordlessly.

I turned the bay into a racing turn to the right. He swept belly-down along the contour of the hillside.

Circle your wagons, Junior.

But don't be fool enough to hold to any one direction for very long, Carl. Huh-uh. Don't let him key those things in front of you.

I pulled the bay to a stop, wheeled him, and showed Junior the finger as another of his mines went off where I would have been.

I gave Junior half of a heartbeat to decide where to punch out the next blast, then spun the horse back on his hocks and sprinted up the slope toward the smoking crater where the last blast had just gone off.

A deadly pattern of rock and gravel erupted above me.

Too far away, thank goodness, but only marginally so. We seemed to have reached the third level of Junior's monster mines. The geysers, then the dirt spray, and now the rocks. I wondered what might be next.

The horse was working hard. I jinked left and left and right and left again, moving in no particular pattern, hoping in that way Junior would not be able to anticipate the next turn.

A series of rapid explosions ripped across the face of the slope above me. He was setting them off in bunches now.

A thumb-sized sliver of stone smacked into my calf, and a good many more must have hit the bay. The horse curvetted and shied, but he was no quitter. I pulled him back under control and pointed him up the hillside toward Junior's home base.

Play King of the Mountain with me, you little bastard. I'll pull you off it and turn your head into a red pulp.

I ran the horse uphill for three jumps, then stopped him and spun to the left. Half of the damn hillside rose up in a spray of dark earth and rock, and the blast was thunderous. It was a hell of a thing to ask the bay horse to face it, but he moved again under my urging.

We were immediately below Junior's Datsun now, and I guided the horse straight uphill toward it. Junior must have been expecting another turn, because I heard a blast to the rear.

The ground was flatter here near the top, and the bay stretched out into a hard, belly-down run toward the little car.

I leaned and twitched my makeshift rein to bring the horse around to the right, in front of the Datsun, and Junior touched off another of his charges practically under his own car. I thought I saw a glint of metal in the shards of homemade shrapnel that were flying.

The horse shied slightly from the explosion and turned back to the left.

We were at the car now, and Junior was just beyond, but the bay was still racing flat out as hard as he could go.

Damn, I thought, and braced myself for the impact when the horse would run into the damn car. I was ready to go over the bay's head and end up on the ground beyond the car.

Instead the bay lifted gracefully into the air and sailed over the hood of the little car like it was just another barrier in the show ring.

Junior's perch was only a matter of yards away now. He was close enough that I could see the panic in his eyes.

He jammed his palm down onto the control box, and all around us the earth shook and trembled as his remaining charges blew at one time.

We were inside the circle of his game now, though, and it was too late for him to take me with his electronic toy.

The horse was on him, and I launched myself off the animal's back at full gallop.

Junior Goodroe came down from the top of his mountain with his face grinding into the spiky gravel soil and the control box tumbling out of his grasp.

I came up straddling him and raised a clubbed fist intent on smashing him. I was breathing hard and I was mad, and the urge was in me to destroy him.

Somewhere I found the strength to put a brake on it. My fist hung there, and after a moment I knew I could not use it.

He wasn't worth that.

I pulled him to his feet and began hauling him down the hillside toward his car.

36

Glen Goodroe looked ten years older than when I had walked into his office a few weeks before. He rubbed at the dark circles under his eyes and motioned me to a chair. We were in the family room, and I felt more than a little uncomfortable about being back in this house again.

"I . . . we . . . owe you a great deal, Carl."

I began to protest, but he cut me short. "Please."

I shrugged.

"Ju . . ." He looked apologetic and almost smiled. "*Glen*. The doctor tells me it is important that we begin calling him Glen. He resents being called Junior." The man sighed. "Glen resents a great many things, it seems."

"Will he be all right?"

"We don't know. If he ever is . . . all right again . . . it would be a very long time from now."

I nodded.

"So much resentment. So much I never suspected. If only . . ." He shook his head. "It is much too late to think about all the things that might have happened 'if.'" He looked immeasurably sad. "Glen has been talking quite freely, Carl. I thought you might want to know."

"Of course." I didn't particularly, but I thought Glen Senior might need to talk, and the Lord knew, there would be damn few people he could ever discuss any of this with.

"Glen was resentful of so many things. He saw this as a way to strike back at me. Naturally Haloran would have been delighted to get my Rainbow Drive. He approached them, and they jumped at the opportunity."

Goodroe looked quite grim. "There will be certain discussions with the Haloran home office. I strongly suspect

163

there will be punitive actions taken and a certain number
of careers curtailed.''

That I did not doubt. Not after hearing the steel in Glen
Goodroe's voice, I didn't.

"That . . . *man* over there apparently recognized what
he was dealing with and was smart enough to feed Junior's
ego.''

I didn't correct his slip about the name. It would take
him some time to get used to it.

"They promised him that when they took over G&G,
Junior would become the president of the division." Glen
snorted. "Take it over. Bullshit. They had no intention of
that and couldn't have accomplished it even if they wanted
to. But he didn't know that. What they wanted, of course,
was the patent on the Rainbow hardware. They had no
interest whatsoever in our software business.

"At any rate, they were smart enough to feed the boy's
ego and capitalize on his . . . problems.''

I couldn't be amazed by that. There are a gracious
plenty of creeps in this world. If he hadn't found some at
Haloran, Junior would have had others to choose from.

Glen was shaking his head. "All that concern I had
about industrial espionage and electronic eavesdropping,
and the whole time it was my own son walking in and out
with any secrets he wanted to carry away. When you came
on the scene, they weren't particularly worried until they
thought you were onto them that afternoon you had decided to go home.''

That brought my eyebrows up a notch. I damn sure
hadn't been onto anybody, more's the pity.

"Apparently you stopped in a lounge before you went to
the restaurant to meet me.''

"Yeah, I was early. I was killing some time.''

"Henry Blair's Haloran contact Wallace Krem was there
waiting for Blair to meet him. You had been described to
him. He thought you were watching him.''

I shook my head. Having a beer isn't always as simple
as it might be.

"He called Junior, I mean Glen, and found out where to
tell Blair to find you. They thought that would discourage

any more favors for old friends. After that . . ." He shrugged.

Yeah. What more was there to say?

"I hope your boy will be all right, Glen."

"He will. Eventually." He gave me a grim smile. "He is fairly happy there, actually. They have some video games in the rec room."

That would be enough to keep him content, I thought.

"There won't be any legal charges against him, will there, Glen?"

"Not unless I file them myself. I'm not likely to do that."

"No."

"Incidentally, I had an interesting telephone call the other day. Do you remember the subdivision they are developing near my expansion site?"

"I think so."

"The man who is doing the foundation work out there called. He was quite angry. I had asked him to do my groundwork when I build out there. He called to find out who I had hired instead."

"I didn't think you were ready to build yet."

"I'm not. He heard all that blasting and assumed there was a construction crew working on it."

I nodded. "That explains why the police never showed up."

"Thank goodness," Glen said with more feeling than he had shown before.

Yeah. It was all right for Junior to try to kill me, just so long as the kid didn't get into trouble with the law. Oh, well. I guess I couldn't blame the man. Sort of.

He reached into his pocket without having to be prompted, which was something of a relief. Under the circumstances I would have found it awkward to have to remind the man that he had promised to contribute to the Heller bank account. Not impossible, mind, but definitely awkward.

The check he handed me was what I believe a banker would call "substantial." Enough to pay for a blown-apart Jeep CJ7 several times over and leave something extra for throwing-away purposes.

I really did not feel like sitting around talking to him

any longer and reminding him of his misery. It was beginning to feel contagious anyway. "Look, Glen, if you don't
need me here anymore, I have some shopping to do. Pick
up some things for the new Jeep and all. . . ." Which was
true enough. The new one Spike had found for me would
not feel like it was mine until I had it tailored to my own
wants and tickles.

Goodroe just continued to sit where he was. I am not
even sure that he heard me. I backed away and headed out
of the room feeling almost sorry that I'd been successful in
preserving his valuable Rainbow Drive.

Sandy met me at the front door with my coat. She had
answered the doorbell, then promptly disappeared.

"You are a nice man, Carl Heller," she said. Shyly, I
thought.

"You're a nice lady, Alexandra." I pulled the coat on.

"When you first got here . . ."

"Mmmm?"

"I was making comparisons. Between you and my ex.
He was, well, he was a bum. Charming but a bum. Your
life-style sounded like more of the same. When you . . .
when we kissed that one time . . . I kept thinking about
that. I didn't want to make the same mistake a second
time. Do you understand what I'm trying to tell you?"

I smiled at her. "I think so. It's all right, you know." I
touched her cheek. "Sometime, when you're feeling up to
it, I wouldn't mind having dinner with you again. Just for
the pleasure of it."

She smiled back. "Sure. Sometime." She came up onto
her tiptoes and gave me a chaste peck on the side of the
jaw.

Light as it was, I could still feel that brief touch as I
walked out the door. It was cold out there. The wind
coming down off the mountains to the west carried the
crisp, sharp smell of distant snow.

But I was wondering how much of the cold I was
feeling had to do with the wind. And how much did not.

I zipped my coat closed to the throat, but that didn't
make me feel any warmer.

ABOUT FRANK RODERUS

Like so many of my generation, and just like the song says, "my heroes have always been cowboys." I have a deep and abiding love for the American West, what it taught us, and what it stands for. But not until I moved into the high country, far from grocery stores and modern services, did I realize how very much alive the spirit of the West truly is.

Carl Heller is a product of imagination. But he could as easily be friend and neighbor.

Here where addresses are given in terms of direction from ranches and valleys, creeks and mountain peaks, the people are independent of spirit and free to rise or fall on the basis of the strengths God has granted them. Carl Heller is, quite simply, one of them.

The situations he finds himself in are taken from the newspaper headlines of today and of tomorrow. They are a part of the daily fabric of the modern West. Some of them have already happened; all of them could happen.

And like any good friend, Carl and I share many interests, many loves. We both appreciate the feel of a strong-running motorcycle swooping the curves of Ute Pass or Florissant Canyon. We both are enamored of the American Quarter Horse with its great heart and quick feet. We both dote on the brisk, clean air and the magnificent vistas of the West. In one respect I have been more fortunate than Carl, because I have a family with whom I can share these pleasures. Carl, though, is basically a friend and neighbor with whom I would be glad to share my hunting camp.

Don't miss the next thrilling
Carl Heller adventure:

THE
TURN-OUT
MAN

by Frank Roderus

They were young, not much older than girls, really. Maybe not so innocent, but certainly unprepared for being "turned out" into the hell of the prostitution/porno underground in Reno. The whole girl-trade pipeline made Heller sick. Trying to shut it down could get him killed.

Available February 1, 1985,
wherever Bantam Books are sold.

THE THRILLING AND MASTERFUL NOVELS OF ROSS MACDONALD

Winner of the Mystery Writers of America Grand Master Award, Ross Macdonald is acknowledged around the world as one of the greatest mystery writers of our time. *The New York Times* has called his books featuring private investigator Lew Archer "the finest series of detective novels ever written by an American."

Now, Bantam Books is reissuing Macdonald's finest work in handsome new paperback editions. Look for these books (a new title will be published every month) wherever paperbacks are sold or use the handy coupon below for ordering: